NEAR MISS

The Colt roared and spat its hot lead from Clint's fist. Although he could smell the acrid smoke, Clint didn't see the first hint of blood from Raven. In fact, he didn't even see the other man standing where he'd been no less than a second ago.

Where Raven had been facing Clint before, he was now twisted to the side. The front of his shirt had a fresh tear going across his belly where the Colt's bullet had traveled. He'd moved so fast that Clint had missed it simply by allowing himself to blink.

Raven shifted his spearlike fingers to point at Clint's eyes. He smiled at that moment, anticipating the glory of taking the Gunsmith's life . . .

THE GUNSMITH

263

EMPTY HAND

J. R. ROBERTS

JOVE BOOKS, NEW YORK

EMPTY HAND

A Jove Book / published by arrangement with
the author

PRINTING HISTORY
Jove edition / November 2003

ISBN: 0-515-13634-4

A JOVE BOOK®
Jove Books are published by The Berkley Publishing Group,
a division of Penguin Group (USA) Inc.,
375 Hudson Street, New York, New York 10014.
JOVE and the "J" design
are trademarks belonging to Penguin Group (USA) Inc.

PRINTED IN THE UNITED STATES OF AMERICA

10   9   8   7   6   5   4   3   2   1

ONE

Nothing shattered the tranquillity of a nice, quiet day like gunshots.

No matter how relaxed a man was or what state his mind was in, that distinctive explosive crack would always wake him up quicker than a splash of cold water in the face. It rattled through his ears and struck at something deep inside, stirring up his most primal instincts: fight or run.

Clint Adams had been riding along the Oregon Trail for the past couple of days and had only recently turned south toward California. It had been some time since he'd visited the state of golden promise, which was reason enough for him to head there now. Most of the trip had been uneventful and he'd only run across a few other souls along the way.

This day had seemed to be no different. In fact, there was still nobody else in sight. But it didn't take too much brain power to know that those shots weren't firing themselves.

A sharp snap of the reins was all it took to put some steam into Eclipse's steps. The black Darley Arabian stallion let out a loud snorting breath and began digging his hooves into the soil. The horse's muscles pumped like a steam engine, carrying Clint like a bullet toward the northwest where the last shots had been heard.

By the sound of it, the guns weren't too far away. Clint hunkered down and let his arms and torso move with the horse beneath him until they almost became one living thing. Clint's attention quickly focused on what was ahead as another ripple of gunshots cracked through the air.

He was just about to touch his heels to the Darley Arabian's sides when Clint caught sight of a trace of smoke rising up from behind a sparse outcropping of rock surrounded by a few gangly trees. There were a couple horses standing outside the perimeter of trees, and all of the riders were currently on foot. Clint counted four horses, but that didn't mean that there were no others about.

The gunshots were already beginning to taper off, which made Clint wonder if he'd just stumbled upon a hunting party that was closing in on its prey. Just as he was about to pull back on Eclipse's reins so as not to scare away whatever game the hunters were after, he saw a single figure burst out from between two rocks. The figure ran like a rabbit that had been flushed from its hole, but moved on two legs.

Another man poked his head out from between those same rocks and shouted something over his shoulder. After that, he lifted a rifle to his shoulder, sighted down the barrel and squeezed off a shot.

That was all Clint had to see before he coaxed even more speed from Eclipse and steered the Darley Arabian toward the first fleeing man.

The stallion closed the distance between it and the one on foot in a matter of seconds. Apparently, that was just enough time for the remaining hunters to break from cover and start in with a fresh round of gunfire. Their rifles sent lead blazing through the air, each round hissing like a deadly insect as Clint got closer and closer.

Clint cursed to himself as another round of shots was thrown toward the running man. He felt as though he could see the bullets' trail as they tore through the air and headed toward the fleeing figure. As he got closer, though, Clint couldn't see any sign that the running man had been hit or even hurt much at all. There was no blood on the tanned hides he wore and he moved quick enough to widen the gap between himself and the men on his tail.

That solitary figure streaked through the short, dead grass with such speed that it seemed impossible that he used only two legs instead of four. He leapt over ruts and rocks with ease, springing just high enough to clear the obstructions without breaking his stride.

Watching the lithe figure move, Clint had to wonder how those riflemen had gotten this close to him in the first place.

So far, it still seemed as though none of the men had spotted him as Clint rode into the fray without wasting a moment to think about the bullets whipping by around him. Before he took Eclipse directly into the line of fire, Clint drew his modified Colt and fired a shot toward the hunters and high over their heads.

The gunshot stopped the hunters dead in their tracks and they looked over at Clint with stunned surprise.

That solitary figure had taken notice of Clint as well. Still moving toward his goal, the lean, dark-skinned man glanced first at Clint and then back to his pursuers.

Now that the shooting had stopped, Clint moved Eclipse between the hunters and their human prey. Although the Colt remained out of its holster, it wasn't aimed directly at any of the armed men. It was, however, resting sideways on the front of his saddle and pointing in the hunters' general direction.

Before too long at all, every one of those four rifles was pointed at Clint. The men wielding them planted their feet, breathing heavily and thankful to be standing still for

a change. None of that gratefulness was spilling over to
Clint, however. They seemed just as ready to shoot him
as they were the dark-skinned man in the distance.

"Step aside, mister," one of the riflemen said. "Or we'll
drop you and move on over your corpse."

TWO

Clint glanced quickly over his shoulder to make sure the dark-skinned man was still there. Although that one bounced lightly from foot to foot as though he was ready to bolt, he was standing his ground. The young man's sharp eyes darted back and forth between Clint and the others, who were fanning out to try and draw a bead on their original target.

Since it was plain to see that the dark-skinned man wasn't about to go anywhere for the moment, Clint turned his attention back to the four riflemen. "Mind if I ask what you men are doing here?" Clint said.

The rifleman who'd done the talking before took a step forward. He stood about average height, which was only slightly shorter than the other three around him. His face was creased with deep lines, which made his skin resemble worn leather. A bristly mustache covered his upper lip and was the same dark brown as the close-cropped hair on his head.

"I'm Jake Riley," the rifleman said.

Clint waited for a moment When it became obvious that nothing else was coming by way of explanation, he asked, "Should that mean anything to me?"

Riley sneered. "It would if you were from around here."

"Well, I'm not, so it doesn't." Clint was happy to cool the situation down slightly just by breaking up the chase. He'd been hoping to give the other man a chance to run, but the dark-skinned man didn't seem to be the least bit interested in running anywhere anymore.

Rather than take advantage of the distraction, the man in the tanned hides merely kept Clint between himself and the riflemen. He kept low and crouched down. His hands brushed along the top of the grass, but kept well above the ground. That posture gave him an almost feral appearance. All the while, his eyes took in everything that was going on.

Although Riley seemed more than a little annoyed at where Clint was standing, he didn't let himself get too worked up about it. "Well, since you don't know me and we don't know you, how about you just keep your nose out of things that don't concern you?"

"Normally, I'd be happy to step aside and let you go about your business, but I don't like the looks of this hunting party. Especially since it seems like you're hunting an unarmed man."

"Unarmed, hell!" one of the other riflemen spat out. "That redskin's a killer and a goddamn savage!"

"Then turn him over to the law," Clint said. "If you run him down and put a bullet through his skull, that makes you killers as well. Killers and savages."

Clint could see that his last comment cut down to the quick on all the riflemen except for Riley. The men flanking Riley were younger, and worked up after getting the taste of gunpowder in their throats and chasing after their quarry like a pack of dogs.

"You don't know what you're talkin' about, mister," the most angered of the riflemen said. His hair was the color of dirty straw, which made the flush in his cheeks seem even redder by comparison. "You don't know what that Injun is and what he's done. If'n you did, you'd be after him just like we—"

"Shut up, Andy," Riley interrupted. "This one here doesn't know our business and he doesn't need to know. What he does need to know is when to step aside and let folks get *on* with their business."

"I'll be more than happy to move along," Clint replied. "In fact, I think I'd be more than happy to do that right now."

Whatever relief the riflemen felt was short-lived as Clint pointed his Colt from where it was laying over his saddle and squeezed off two quick shots followed by a third and fourth. The first two shots were aimed at Andy and the other rifleman standing right next to him. Both of those men winced in pain and dropped to the ground as though their bodies were suddenly too heavy for their legs to bear.

The second pair of shots fired from Clint's gun headed toward Riley and the other man next to him. A mound of dirt was kicked up at Riley's feet, causing him to jump back a step while the other rifleman felt a sting in his arm and reflexively lowered his weapon.

Clint was already moving the instant he'd fired his fourth shot. Pulling back on the reins, he turned Eclipse around and headed back toward the dark-skinned man behind him. He wrapped the reins around his gun hand and reached down with his other hand so he could offer it to the other figure crouching low to the ground.

"Now's your chance," Clint said.

The dark-skinned man wasted no time at all before taking hold of Clint's hand and allowing himself to be pulled up onto Eclipse's back. He swung his leg over the Darley Arabian and twisted his body around so that he could land directly behind Clint, ready to go.

Clint felt the other man's hand in his grasp, but felt as though he did hardly anything else to help him onto the saddle. With just a minimal pull, Clint saw the other man rise up off the ground and spring onto Eclipse as though something had picked him up and set him down again.

There wasn't enough time to admire the other man's grace, however, so Clint snapped the reins and got the stallion running away from the riflemen. He twisted around to look at the men he'd left behind and was just in time to see Andy lift his rifle and take a shot at him.

The rifle went off quickly, which was exactly what Clint had expected. That reason alone was why he'd taken a shot at that man first. It was also why he did a little more damage to Andy than he had to any of the others. He didn't take the extra time to study where his bullets had gone, but Clint was confident enough in his own ability that he knew he'd hit Andy in the meaty portion of his upper arm. That wound would hurt like a bastard and, more importantly, would affect his aim.

The others, however, wouldn't have as much trouble once they started to fire.

"I thank you," the dark-skinned man said.

Clint let out a quick laugh. "Well, don't thank me yet." With that, he reached around and shoved the man behind him off Eclipse's back before bringing the stallion around to charge toward the rifles.

THREE

Before Eclipse could get too much closer to the angered shooters, Clint steered the Darley Arabian in another direction so he could run around the riflemen altogether. Once he was certain Eclipse knew where he was going, Clint swung one leg over the saddle and launched himself off the horse's back completely.

For a moment, Clint felt the wind wrapping around him as he sailed through the air. That moment was very brief, however, and ended abruptly when his feet slammed against the ground and his body dropped down on top of them. Although it could have been a little more graceful, the maneuver was successful enough to get him off Eclipse's back without breaking his legs in the process.

Clint's body was still falling forward when he leaned into his own momentum and tucked his chin tightly against his chest. He had just managed to pull his arms in tightly to his sides when he fell into a forward roll, which carried him about ten feet from where he'd landed. Once there, he stuck out one leg to stop himself and let his momentum push him onto his feet.

At first, he thought he'd managed to pull off the maneuver and end up in a standing position. But he quickly felt that his body wanted to keep going, and he swung his arms in front of him to brace for impact. Clint's knees bent and he landed on all fours, feeling slightly foolish for making the awkward stumble.

That feeling evaporated as soon as he heard the rifle shots crack through the air and bullets hiss over his head. As awkward and slightly painful as the landing had been, dropping down to hands and knees had managed to keep him from taking at least one round in the head.

Clint took a moment to count his blessings before pulling his legs up under him and preparing to lift himself back up again. Before he did that, he had to check one thing. Clint's hand dropped down to the holster at his side, patting the leather bundle to make sure that it wasn't empty.

The last time he'd thought about the Colt, it had been in his hand. Apparently, he didn't have to think before dropping it back into its holster because the gun was there when Clint checked. It took less than a second for his mind to recall that even though the pistol was still in his possession, it only had two rounds left in the cylinder.

Every one of Clint's instincts were screaming for him to draw the Colt and send both of those remaining shots back at the riflemen. As difficult as it was, he kept those impulses in check and lifted his empty hands into the air.

"This doesn't have to go any further," Clint said. "I just can't stand by and watch you execute an unarmed man."

"We don't give a shit what you can stand," Andy shouted. His voice was tainted by pain and anger. Even with the distance between them, Clint could see the way the younger man bared his teeth when he spoke. "And you've already pushed this too far."

Clint saw the dark bloodstains on two of the men's shirts, but noticed that all four of them were up and moving. "We can all walk away from this with the scratches we've already taken. If I hear from the law that that man's a killer, I'll help you track him down myself."

Saying those words, Clint felt as though it hadn't been too long since he'd heard similar things come out of his mouth. In fact, he'd stepped into the middle of a manhunt not too long ago. Thinking back to that instance, Clint wondered if he should have just taken Riley's advice and minded his own business.

Too late for that now, though. Hopefully this would turn out better than that other situation had.

Andy seemed only too eager to take another shot at Clint, but he was stopped by a firm grip on his shoulder. It was Riley holding him back, and the more aggressive younger man barely managed to obey the silent command he'd just been given.

Stepping forward, Riley pushed Andy's rifle down until it was aimed at the ground. "I admire your gumption," he said to Clint. "But we've got a job to do and we don't have the time to explain ourselves to just anyone we come across. What my men need to remember is that we're not after you or yours, so we just need to wrap up our business and be on our way."

"As long as that business doesn't include murder, I don't have a problem with that," Clint said.

Riley nodded and said, "Funny thing is how hard you're trying to get that Injun away from us."

"Why is that so funny?"

"Because he doesn't seem interested in taking your good advice."

Clint could see that Riley was looking at something in the distance. The only reason he took a look for himself was that he hadn't seen the dark-skinned man take one step away from the area since he'd dropped him off a minute or two ago.

Glancing over his shoulder, Clint made sure to keep Andy and the others in his peripheral vision. Sure enough, the dark-skinned man was still standing there. In fact, he seemed to have his back straight and his chest puffed out as though he was posing for a statue.

Clint caught a hint of movement coming from the riflemen and swung around to look at them head-on. He was just in time to see one of them lift his weapon as if to take aim at Clint. Before Clint could react, Andy leapt forward as well, swinging his rifle like a club aimed at Clint's knees.

Twisting to one side, Clint lifted one leg and allowed Andy's swing to pass by without crashing into him. He took hold of the first man's rifle by the barrel, pulled it forward and jerked that one off his balance. Besides putting the advantage back onto himself, Clint also managed to get that man's chin a foot or two closer. He swung his free hand in a sharp hook, his fist impacting solidly.

A shot went off directly beside Clint, and when he spun around to look, he saw that Riley had been the one to pull the trigger. The Colt was already filling Clint's fist and the pistol's barrel was already aimed at Riley's head. The only thing keeping him from pulling the trigger was that Riley's gun was not aimed at him.

Instead, Riley had taken a shot in the opposite direction, where the dark-skinned man was still standing proudly in the distance. That one shot seemed to echo and roll through Clint's ears twice as long as any of the others. It did that mainly because that had been the one shot that he'd been trying most to prevent.

At that moment, he would have rather felt the lead chew into his own body. Wherever he went, people were taking shots at him anyway, and every once in a while one of them got lucky. Clint had been shot plenty of times and no longer feared it as much as he probably should. But this time, he'd been fighting to keep that dark-skinned man alive and healthy.

Now it seemed as though all of that effort and risk might have been for nothing.

Clint looked out toward the figure in the distance, and his hopes grew brighter as that man stayed on his feet. Perhaps Riley had missed and there was still time to calm the situation down before a life was lost. But those hopes were quickly extinguished when the dark-skinned man crumpled over and dropped like a sack of grain.

Lowering the rifle from his shoulder, Riley said, "All right, boys. This has been a misunderstanding. Let's collect the Injun's carcass and be on our way. I'm sure our friend here has some more good deeds to do."

FOUR

Andy and the other man Clint had grazed with his first two shots clutched their wounds and glared at him with open contempt. They kept their eyes on him, but followed Riley's lead. Both of them had their fingers tight around their triggers, waiting for an excuse to even their score. Even as they itched to finish the fight that had been interrupted, all three of the other men moved past Clint and walked behind Riley.

For the moment, Clint watched as the riflemen headed toward the spot where the dark-skinned man had fallen. Once they'd all moved on, he brought up the rear and followed them all while quietly reloading his pistol.

The air seemed especially quiet. It was the dead of winter, but there had been a bit of a warm snap which had gotten rid of most of the snow that had covered the ground. The cold had returned, but it wasn't powerful enough to be too uncomfortable.

Since they'd all had plenty of time to accustom themselves to the change of seasons, none of the men were hampered by the temperatures, which were once again falling to expected lows. As on all cold days, the sound just didn't carry as far as it did in the heat. It would have

14

been quiet no matter what, but under the circumstances the entire area seemed to have been turned into a tomb.

Clint could hear every blade of grass crunching beneath the feet of the procession. Knowing that he'd already accomplished his goal, Riley wasn't in any particular hurry to get where he was going. In fact, he appeared to be savoring the walk over to the fallen man's body, since he'd dropped his prey despite Clint's best efforts to stop him.

After the Colt was fully loaded, Clint dropped the pistol back into its holster. He closed some of the distance between himself and the riflemen, but decided to hang back enough so that none of the others could launch any kind of attack.

Not too far away, Eclipse began trotting toward Clint from the spot where he'd been waiting. The Darley Arabian stopped immediately, however, when he saw Clint give him a quick wave and a stern look. As soon as Clint turned to once again face the riflemen, the stallion walked slowly to keep up with the others.

Clint could smell the gunpowder in the air and felt the cold biting into him more than ever. The closer he got to where the body was laying, the more he wanted to do something about it. But what galled him the most was that it appeared to be too late for him to do anything that would do anyone any good at all.

After another minute had passed, Riley was the first one to stop. He looked down at the ground with such satisfaction that Clint didn't have to see what he was looking at. Waving to the others, Riley formed a circle around his find and glanced up at Clint.

"You still here?" Riley asked.

Clint didn't answer. Instead, he took another step closer, until he could see the form lying motionless in the middle of all four men. Now that the figure was no longer moving, Clint could make out the skins worn by the fallen man. They were smooth and form-fitting, marked with Indian symbols that had been worn into the leather after years of painting.

All Clint could see was one leg and an arm since the man on the ground had rolled onto his side after dropping. Riley stared down at the body and nodded solemnly. Andy cleared his throat, brought up a mouthful of slime and spat it onto the still form.

"Really proud of yourself, huh?" Clint asked.

Andy looked up at him, but didn't say a word. The smug grin on his face did all of his talking for him.

Clint glanced at each of the four men in turn. "I'll be looking into this on my own. If your're as well known as you seem to think you are, I shouldn't have much trouble seeing what this was all about."

"Go right ahead," Riley said. "We got nothin' to hide. Besides, can't you see this is just an Injun? It doesn't matter who he is or what he's done; I could get a reward for shooting him from half the soldiers within a hundred miles."

Although Clint knew the government wasn't officially supportive of killing natives anymore, he knew the real world rarely kept itself in line with what was official. Riley was correct in what he'd said. Most soldiers in any cavalry unit had seen enough conflict against the tribes that they considered it to be forever open season on all Indian Nations.

It didn't matter that there were plenty of good men in uniform who didn't condone outright murder against anyone with the wrong color skin. All it took was a few that did to encourage men like Riley in whatever savage hunts they could think of.

Thinking about that made Clint's stomach clench and his hands curl into fists. What made him even madder was the fact that he had been unable to save this one man from being shot down like some kind of game animal.

"I don't know what's got you so twisted up over this," Riley said. "But believe me that this redskin had it coming. He's a damn killer, mister. The only thing we did here today was save the good people from wasting their time at a trial and their rope for a hanging.

"In fact, I won't even set the law on you for shooting at my men here. Looks like they only took a scratch or so. Why don't we just part ways and forget about ever meeting up?"

Andy wiped some excess spittle from his chin and stretched out his arm, which was still bleeding from where Clint's bullet had dug into him.

The wound was even smaller than Clint had thought, and that particular revelation was not at all welcome in his mind.

"You wanna watch while we scalp 'im?" Andy asked.

Clint didn't feel the need to say anything in response to that. Even though he'd given the dark-skinned man every chance in the world to get away, Clint felt as if he'd failed.

Just as he was about to keep the four from desecrating the body as well, Clint was distracted by a sudden burst of movement. What shocked the words right out of him was the fact that it was the fallen man's body that was doing the moving.

FIVE

In the blink of an eye, the man on the ground pulled one leg up tight against his chest as though it was an arrow being pulled against a bow. Pressing his hands flat against the ground, he angled his lower body upward and snapped the bent leg straight out toward the closest available target.

Since he'd been taking so much pleasure in lording over the body, it was Andy who was closest to the fallen man and it was his knee that was snapped sideways when the other man's foot slammed into it. Andy let out a pained screech and his eyes went wide as saucers. The sound of his bones cracking apart could still be heard over his agonized cries.

Andy toppled over as if he'd been hit by a cannonball, and before his body hit the ground, the dark-skinned man sprung up and onto his feet. Now that he was close and upright, the dark-skinned man could be seen as something more than a blur of motion or a figure in the distance.

Clint took a second to take a look at the man dressed in weathered skins, and the first thing he noticed was the fact that there wasn't a gunshot wound anywhere on him. Besides that, the man looked to be in his late twenties and had the lean, chiseled face of an animal made strong after years of fighting for its life.

The man's features were definitely Indian, as was his thick, raven black hair that hung down well past his shoulders. His eyes were so dark that they almost seemed black as well, and they burned with a primal fire that still could not hide the intelligence within. Smooth, dark skin was marred by the occasional scar, and when he opened his mouth to let out a warrior's cry, he displayed sharp, almost canine, teeth.

Clint took all of that in within the space of half a second. After that, it was hard to see much of anything else about the Indian because he was once again launching into a blindingly swift movement.

"Son of a bitch!" Riley snarled. "Kill this damn Injun!"

Riley and the other two riflemen that were still on their feet lifted their weapons, but didn't get them up more than halfway before the Indian was there to deal with them. The dark-skinned man snapped one hand out to take hold of the closest rifle barrel, and he hung onto that while twisting his body around in a tight spiral.

A three-quarter turn allowed the Indian to pluck the rifle from one man's hand and line him up to bury his moccasined foot in Riley's gut. The kick drove in so deep that Clint wouldn't have been surprised to see the Indian's foot come out through Riley's back. It did, however, crumple Riley over and send every bit of air from his lungs in a wheezing gasp.

The Indian pulled his foot back and cocked it once again against his chest. From there, he snapped it straight out and hooked it around so his heel pounded against the third man's jaw. That one dropped his rifle and staggered back, bringing both hands up to grab hold of his aching face.

For a moment, Clint watched all of this in disbelief. The Indian moved so fast and with such precision that

Clint was almost having trouble taking it all in. He didn't have any trouble at all spotting Andy on the ground reaching for a pistol that had been tucked beneath his belt. Noticing that the Indian was facing away from Andy, Clint knew that he had about a second to act before the dark-skinned man was put down for real.

Clint took one step forward, set his foot down right behind Andy and swung his other foot straight out to deliver a swift kick to Andy's chin. Although he didn't put all of his strength behind the blow, Clint could tell he'd gotten the job done when Andy's head snapped back and to the side. The younger man's eyes were glazed over when he looked back at Clint and fell over into unconsciousness.

All this time, the Indian hadn't stopped moving. Still gripping the rifle he'd taken by the barrel, he swung it like a club over his head and into the face of the man he'd taken it from. Confident that he'd put that one away, the Indian turned his attention to one of the two that remained.

Since Riley was still trying to catch his breath, the Indian looked over to the rifleman who he'd kicked in the jaw. He moved as though he had all the time in the world to plot out his actions, jabbing the rifle straight into the other man's gut and then snapping one foot up into his chest. The move knocked that man flat onto his back, leaving only Riley as a concern.

Riley started to say something, but the words only sounded like guttural snarls coming from the back of his throat. Apparently, he was too busy getting ready to fire his gun to be overly concerned with making comments about it. He held the rifle in both hands and levered in a round without taking more than a second.

Even though Riley was quick, the Indian was still quicker as he spun around in another tight circle and dropped down to the ground. His entire body twisted three

hundred and sixty degrees while he supported his weight
upon one hand. As soon as his head came around for him
to lock eyes with Riley, the Indian straightened out the
leg that was swinging around like a log wrapped in tanned
leather.

His leg sliced just above the short grass like a wheel
spinning on its axel. The back of his heel caught the back
of Riley's leg, sweeping the other man's support right out
from under him. Once that was done, the rest of Riley's
body came tumbling down as well and the Indian was
springing back up onto his feet.

When he hit the dirt, Riley rolled back and forth
slightly, trying desperately to pull some air into his lungs.
Looking up at the sky, he was just in time to see the
Indian looming over him with the stolen rifle held in front
of him.

"If you're gonna shoot, go on and do it," Riley said.
Looking over to Clint, he added, "I'm glad you're watching this, mister. Now you can see what kind of a savage
we're dealing with. I hope you're ready to put this dog
down before he kills me."

Clint looked back and forth from Riley to the Indian.
The strange thing was that the dark-skinned man seemed
much calmer than any of the others laying on the ground.
For a man who'd just dropped four armed men in a matter
of a few seconds, the Indian seemed downright casual
about the whole thing.

Returning Clint's gaze, the Indian nodded once and
then jumped straight up into the air. The movement was
as quiet as it was quick. One moment he was standing
there and the next, he was hanging a foot or so over Riley's torso.

Acting as though gravity just didn't affect him the way
it did any other man, the Indian brought both legs up a
bit, shifted his weight and dropped down onto Riley's gut.
The impact doubled the man like a jackknife, but the In-

dian was up and bouncing off to one side before Riley had started convulsing.

The Indian landed lightly on the ground and straightened his back until he was once again standing proud and tall amid his fallen pursuers. Riley was still trying to talk, but this time he didn't have the air or strength to get out more than a strained cough.

While watching the entire scene play out before him, Clint had been waiting for the Indian to do something out of line. Considering the fact that he'd been unarmed and chased down like a dog, Clint figured it was only fair to let the dark-skinned man get in a few licks of his own. He'd been ready to step in if it seemed as though anyone's life was in jeopardy, but the only ones who'd been ready to kill were Riley and his men.

Now that the dust was settling, Clint squared off with the Indian and let his hands hang empty at his sides. He met the Indian's gaze and immediately felt the intensity within those dark eyes.

Slowly, the Indian extended his arms and held the rifle out in front of him. "I am no savage," he said, before opening his hands and letting the weapon drop to the ground.

SIX

Clint stepped forward and didn't feel the slightest need to worry when he got within the Indian's striking distance. Even after all he'd seen from the dark-skinned man, and the speed with which he'd fought, something within Clint's instincts told him that the storm had passed. At least, the storm had passed for the moment, anyway.

Giving the Indian some breathing room, Clint walked over to each of the riflemen and took their weapons from them one by one. He started with the ones who were still conscious and also made sure to search them quickly for any holdout guns or knives. They each had something in reserve and Clint tossed them all into a pile about ten feet away.

He then went to each of the men and looked him over to find out the extent of his wounds. Even though Clint was no doctor, he'd seen more than his share of brawls and could tell a serious wound from one that just hurt like hell. All of the ones he found fell into the latter category, and none of the riflemen would take home any permanent injuries.

Of course, after the time spent with Jake Riley and his crew, Clint wouldn't have been too bent out of shape if

they'd been busted up a little more. The fact that they
weren't told him an awful lot about the dark-skinned man
standing in front of him.

Clint started to offer his greeting to the Indian, but was
cut off when the other man turned and dashed off toward
the trail that had brought Clint to this area in the first
place. After running ten yards or so, the Indian stopped
and motioned for Clint to follow him. He didn't wait for
an answer to his invitation before turning and running off
once again.

All it took was a quick whistle for Clint to call over
Eclipse, who'd been waiting not too far away. The Darley
Arabian trotted over to Clint's side and waited until he
felt the familiar weight on his back.

Now sitting in the saddle, Clint snapped his reins and
rode to catch up with the Indian, who was still running
like a jackrabbit toward a cluster of boulders about a quarter of a mile away. Even with the stallion doing the running, it took a surprising amount of effort to catch up with
the Indian. Eclipse didn't have any trouble at all com-
pleting the task, but he would have caught anyone else in
a fraction of the time it took to draw up alongside the
dark-skinned man.

Once he was riding beside the Indian, Clint looked
down and saw the other man acknowledge him with a
quick sideways nod. The Indian kept right on running,
though, and didn't stop until they made it to those rocks.
Coming to a stop behind the boulders, the Indian planted
his feet and straightened his back to become the picture
of pride and strength. As far as Clint could tell, the dark-
skinned man wasn't even breathing heavily.

Clint swung down from the saddle and stood beside
Eclipse. He kept one hand on the stallion's neck and held
out the other one in greeting. "That's a hell of a lot of
exercise for one day, friend," Clint said amiably. "If I
were you, I don't know if I could even stand up."

For a moment, the Indian simply looked down at Clint's hand as though he thought it might bite him. Before too long, the sternness in his features subsided a bit and he accepted Clint's handshake. "I stand because I don't allow myself to tire. It is the only way for me to travel as I do."

"You could always saddle a horse to do some of that running for you."

"But then I would move too fast to see and I would not feel the land pass below my own feet."

"True," Clint said with a shrug. "And you'd also miss out on meeting fine company like those four back there."

Clint's comment was met with stony silence for a moment. The wintry chill in the air seemed to get just a little colder as the Indian stared straight into Clint's eyes. Then, suddenly, his face broke into a wide smile and his shoulders shook with laughter.

"My name is Clint Adams."

"And I am called Motega."

"Motega? That sounds Mexican."

"It isn't. My people are from tribes scattered throughout this land. I have the blood of Chinook and Nez Percé flowing through my veins, and though I am not fully a part of one tribe, I am welcomed by most."

"It's good to have a big family," Clint said. "Especially in hard times."

Those words seemed to pull the smile right off of Motega's face. He drew in a deep breath and nodded slowly. "Hard times, yes. For some men, there are no other times."

Clint let a few moments go by before saying what had really been burning in his mind. "Forgive me for prying," he finally said. "But I'd really like to know exactly what the hell I stumbled into back there. Do you mind filling me in on why those men were running you down like that?"

"To fight, men like that seldom need a reason beyond the color of another man's skin. They are wild and overly confident behind their guns. But then again, without men such as those, I would fall out of practice in my training."

"I'm not about to say I feel sorry for those four," Clint said good-naturedly, "but I still would like to know what happened. Something in my gut tells me that it was more than just a bunch of assholes chasing you for being an Indian."

"There is more, Clint Adams. There is plenty more to be told."

"One of them said you were a murderer. Where would he get that idea?"

As he asked that question, Clint watched the Indian's face very closely. He searched for any hint of how the words affected him, if Motega was hiding something. Motega didn't even flinch at what was said, however, and he didn't try to defend himself right away.

Instead, the Indian let a few moments slip by and then answered, "They got that idea because I had to kill two of the men who used to ride with them."

SEVEN

Clint had met plenty of murderers in his life. One thing that they all had in common was an empty coldness in their eyes. Once a person killed another person, something inside of him died off as well. It didn't matter if he killed that person with good or bad intentions, or even if it had been justified or not.

Once a man had blood on his hands, there was no going back to the way he'd been before. Clint knew that for a fact, since he had blood on his own hands as well. One thing he could also tell was the difference between killers and men who'd killed.

A killer enjoyed what he'd done and wouldn't think too hard about doing it again. A killer didn't lose a wink of sleep over taking another man's life, and he might even be proud of what he'd done. That kind of thing was a little harder to spot within someone's eyes, but it could be seen once you knew what to look for.

Try as he might, Clint couldn't see any of that special kind of wickedness anywhere on the Indian's face. Although that didn't necessarily mean that it wasn't there, it did allow him to listen to what Motega had to say.

There was a town no more than another day's ride away

called Padre's Crossing. Since both men were headed for that town, Clint and Motega decided to travel together. Clint rode while Motega walked, and for the moment, neither one of them seemed in the least bit worried that the four they'd left behind would come after them anytime soon.

"So tell me, Motega," Clint said once they were back on the trail and well on their way. "Why would you have to kill anyone? Were they Indian hunters as well?"

"They were not Indian hunters. The plague of those bloodthirsty dogs was much worse when I was younger."

"The tribes might have seen bloodier days, but their problems aren't exactly over. You and I both know it's not too hard to find payment in return for the right kind of scalps if you know where to look."

Clint knew his words sounded harsh, but that had been another way for him to test Motega. Much as if he was sitting at a poker table with the Indian, he tested the other man in various ways to see how he would react. It was plain to see that Motega felt a sting at hearing Clint's words, but no more so than would have been expected from any other native.

"You don't have to tell me this, Clint Adams. Most of my family now lives in the Spirit World thanks to the bloodthirsty coyotes who wear the blue suits of the white man's army."

"Your family was killed by Indian hunters?"

Motega nodded. "But this is not a new tale in this land. The Trail of Tears stretches much farther than the Cherokee territories, and it is still being walked to this day. Both of my ancestral tribes were wounded by the white man. This is what makes it easier for me to roam so freely."

Suddenly, Clint felt terrible for testing the other man in a way that would dredge up so much sorrow. Even though Motega didn't seem overly angered by the questions, the

Indian's voice had become dark and withdrawn. His eyes stared straight ahead, as though he was looking at horrible images that Clint didn't even want to see.

At that moment, Clint wouldn't have blamed Motega one bit for taking down some piece-of-shit murderer who traded in scalps that had been torn from women and children. Men like that only cared about money, and they saw Indians as something less than human simply because someone else would pay to have them exterminated.

There was a lot of bad blood between the settlers and the tribes. Both sides had made their mistakes, just as both sides had their killers. Clint had heard arguments either way more than once, but the fight itself was a messy one. It was very messy, indeed.

"I'm sorry to hear that," Clint said.

• "I am, too. But I did not kill those men out of revenge for what happened to my family or my people." Blinking a few times in quick succession, Motega lifted his face to the sky and pulled in a breath of cold air. The wind was well below freezing, but it only seemed to energize him as it blew over his thinly covered body. "That is a debt that will be settled another day, and it is one that I am not fighting for on my own.

"The men I killed left me no alternative. They thought to eliminate me so they could keep one of my elders in chains. I tried talking to them like a man, but they spoke back with hate and gunfire. I had no choice but to kill them, Clint Adams. In that, you must believe me."

Looking down at the Indian walking alongside him, Clint felt more confused than when he'd first ridden into the chase. Something about Motega had compelled Clint to throw in on his side even before he'd learned the Indian's name. He still didn't think he'd made a bad decision, but he didn't have anything besides his own instincts to go by.

"Why do you care what I think?" Clint asked. "You

could probably knock me out and get away from me just as quickly as you did those other four."

"Maybe. But I sense something different in you than I have ever encountered in another white man."

"Really? And what's that?"

"I feel like I can trust you, even though every part of me says that doing so would only cost me my own blood. After all, just as you say I could have gotten away from you, I think things could have gone the other way.

"You could have just as easily listened to the words of your own people and joined in on their hunt. And, as you say, Clint Adams, I have a feeling in my gut that says you could have gunned me down before I could take a swing at you."

"First of all," Clint said, "I want to get one thing straight. Those four back there were definitely not my people. And second, I get nervous every time you say my name like that. Either Clint or Adams. I'd thank you if you picked one and stuck with it."

"Very well." Motega thought for a while as he walked, mulling over the proposition like it carried much more weight than it was worth. "How about Clint? Adams sounds like a soldier's name."

"Or a president's?"

"Ha. You do think highly of yourself, don't you?"

EIGHT

"It's been almost two days, Mr. Harden. Don't you think it's about time we sent somebody out to look after them?"

The man who'd asked that question stood in the doorway of a large suite in Padre Crossing's largest brothel. Only one of two French doors was open, looking out onto a long, carpeted hallway which ran the length of the entire building. Sounds filled the place and seeped through the walls, adding music and voices to the perfumed air.

Inside, the room was filled with paintings and furniture that were all influenced by styles coming from the Far East. Oriental lettering was printed on strips of paper hanging next to the doors, and plush, dark red carpets covered the hardwood floors. In the middle of the room was a porcelain bathtub big enough for three to sit comfortably. Since there were currently only two in the tub, they were very comfortable indeed.

Albert Harden was a solidly built man in his fifties with a head covered in bristly gray hair. It was neatly cut on top of his head, forming a mane that flowed directly into a thick, well-maintained beard which left little of his features to be seen. Leaning with his back against the tub and his arms draped along its rim, Harden sat mostly submerged in steaming hot water with a thick cigar clenched between his teeth.

"Did you just interrupt my bath to tell me how to conduct my business?" Harden asked without causing the cigar to waver even slightly.

The slender Chinese girl sitting in the tub facing him stopped what she was doing to look toward the other man as well. She held a sponge in one hand and was moving it over Harden's chest. Her other hand was beneath the level of the water, which wasn't quite high enough to cover her small, pert breasts.

Max Emery was the name of the man standing in the doorway. Once he realized he'd been staring at the Chinese girl's trim, seductive figure, he removed his hat and held it in front of him as though that made everything square. He looked to be somewhere in his thirties and wore a .38-caliber revolver holstered beneath his simple brown suit jacket.

Max was about average size and his light brown hair was just starting to grow past his shoulders. It was well kept, however, giving him the appearance of a sensible man doing his best to look wild. "I would never want to tell you how to run your business, Mr. Harden."

"Good, then don't start now," Harden said, moving his hands up over the Chinese girl's sides. "I'm busy."

"I can see that, but I just wanted to check in with you since it's been a while since Jake took the rest of his boys out to track down that Injun."

Only then did Harden finally decide to take his eyes away from the wet naked body of the girl sitting with him in the tub "Jake Riley isn't back yet?"

Doing his best not to look too frustrated, Max said, "No. And it's almost been two days since he headed out."

"And you haven't heard anything from him or any of the others that went with him?"

"No, sir."

Harden turned his eyes back toward the Chinese girl. Cupping his hands, he drizzled water over her smooth skin and pulled in a lungful of smoke from his cigar. "All right then," he said before too long. "Tell Abe to track down Jake and the rest so he can find out if they've managed to bag that redskin or if they're all just picking their asses somewhere. Once he finds out, make sure he comes back and lets me know."

"I'll do that, Mr. Harden."

"Make sure that you're clear about that last part," Harden snarled. "Abe can get thickheaded sometimes, especially when it involves turning away from a fight. I want to know what's going on before this goes any further."

Nodding, Max caught himself staring at the Chinese girl once again. Her long black hair was so wet that it clung to her shoulders and neck like it had been painted there. He said, "You know what Abe's next question will be."

"Yeah. And when he asks it, tell him the answer is yes. He can hunt down the Injun if that job still needs doing. In fact, you can tell him he might get a crack at Jake as well if that asshole couldn't manage to kill me one stinking Indian."

"That should go over pretty well."

"I expect so. Abe never turns down a chance to spill some blood."

"Even if it's his own."

That brought a wary smile to Harden's face as he shook his head. "You got that right, too. Nobody ever accused that boy of being right in the head. At least he does what he's told . . . most of the time, anyway."

Max nodded the same way he'd been doing since the conversation had started. Even though the Chinese girl was only moving a little bit, that was still more than enough to hold his attention way beyond the point when he knew it was welcome. Finally, he caught a glimpse of

Harden staring back at him over the burning cigar.

"You like her so much, you should come back when you're done with this little job I gave you," Harden said. "I pay you enough to indulge every now and then."

Without trying to hide the hunger that was stirring deep inside of him, Max tore his eyes away from the girl's glistening body and placed his hat back on top of his head. "Yes, sir. I might just do that."

"Good. In the meantime, get the hell out of here and shut the door behind you. There's a draft coming in and I'd prefer not to have an audience around just now."

Max turned his back on the tub and stepped through the door. He pulled it shut and remained standing in the hallway until he could hear the sounds of the girl's voice coming from Harden's suite. She sounded just as exotic and enticing as she looked. He didn't have to make out any of the words she was saying to find himself wanting her even more.

He decided that he was most definitely coming back. Just when he thought of waiting until that particular girl was available, Max spotted another Chinese beauty walking down the hall dressed in nothing but a short, silky robe.

Oh yes, he would definitely be coming back.

NINE

Harden leaned back and took the cigar from his mouth. He let his hand hang over the side of the tub and flicked his ashes onto the floor. Shifting slightly beneath the water, he felt his body slide between the legs of the girl who was cleaning his chest and shoulders.

The girl still had a few months to go before she turned twenty, and yet she knew more about pleasing a man than Harden's wife had learned over twenty years of marriage. Of course, the girl had probably earned her life in America by servicing men in several different states, but there was something else that separated this particular girl in Harden's mind.

Unlike his wife or any of the other whores in town, this girl paid attention to him. She only had to be told something once and she would remember it every time he came back to her room. Many times, he didn't have to tell her a damn thing before she took care of needs that he didn't even know he had.

"What's your name, China doll?" Harden asked.

The girl smiled, displaying small, pearl white teeth. "Lei Mai," she said in a voice that was nearly musical.

"Lee May," Harden repeated. When he said her name,

he didn't even try to give it the proper emphasis or pronunciation that she had. He simply spat back the sounds and grinned as though he'd impressed himself with his worldliness. "That's a pretty name."

"Thank you."

"Keep washing like that, China doll. You know how I like it."

She knew very well, indeed. After moving the sponge in a few more circles over his chest, she slipped her hands beneath the water and felt down over his stomach. Harden's body stiffened slightly as he anticipated where her touch would go next.

So as not to disappoint him, Lei Mai moved the sponge along his body and onto his leg. Her other hand eased over his thigh and then traced along the side of his penis, which was becoming more erect by the second. She used only the back of her hand at first, teasing him by running only that over his stiff member, as though the touch had been purely accidental.

Harden let out a satisfied sigh, closed his eyes and let his head fall back against the back of the tub. Even as he felt the girl's fingers glide between his legs, he still thought to lift his cigar to his mouth and take another puff.

"That's the way, China doll," he said while letting out a smoky breath. "Just like that."

Lei Mai slid herself down along his body, until she could rest her knees between his ankles. It was only because of her petite size that she could get that far away from him and still remain inside the tub at all. As she moved, her hands massaged Harden's thighs and hips, her fingers kneading his flesh in a way that worked out every bit of tension inside of him.

She could feel that his cock was rigid and waiting for her. All she had to do was brush her fingers along its base and Harden pushed himself toward her even more. Soon, his feet snaked around her knees and drew her in closer.

Lei Mai smiled and allowed herself to be directed until her body was once again pressed against his.

Once there, she straddled his lap and slid the lips of her vagina up and down along the outside of his cock. Her fingernails scratched through the hair on his chest and she made a contented purring sound in the back of her throat.

"You like that, don't ya?" Harden said while reaching into the water with one hand and groping between her legs. "Then why don't you try this on for size."

As he said that, Harden placed his rigid penis between her legs, moving it back and forth until he found the warm, welcoming opening amid her small patch of pubic hair.

With her toes pressing against the bottom of the tub, Lei Mai lifted herself up just enough to allow him to fit inside of her and then slowly let her body slide down on top of him. Harden's cock slid into her pussy, and she didn't stop moving until she'd lowered herself all the way down and taken him completely inside.

The smile on her face was somewhat forced, but it was genuine. Closing her eyes and leaning back, Lei Mai grabbed hold of the edge of the tub and used her hands and legs to slowly move up and down in the steaming water. She clenched her eyes shut even tighter as she concentrated on the sensation of his rigid column of flesh filling her and rubbing against her sensitive skin.

Harden held onto her hips with both hands, savoring the feel of her lithe, wet body slipping between his fingers as she rode him. Her tight stomach moved beneath the water, expanding and contracting in his grasp. From there, he could feel when she pulled in a sharp breath as he occasionally pumped up into her and she rose up out of the water.

Her small breasts were capped with nipples no wider than a button. Their tips were erect with excitement and pink at the ends. As soon as he noticed that little detail, Harden leaned forward and took one of her nipples in his mouth. He took hold of her other breast and squeezed as he sucked and thrust up into her.

Normally quiet during their lovemaking, Lei Mai let out a little yelp. The feeling of his hard cock pumping into her mixed with the little bit of pain from his teeth gave her an exhilarating rush. In fact, it was one of the few times that she found herself truly enjoying being in his company.

With him buried inside of her, Lei Mai slid her hands along the edge of the tub until her arms were resting on either side of his head. That way, he could lean back and move his mouth from one breast to another, sucking and nibbling her as she squirmed on top of him. She especially enjoyed when he would flick his tongue around her nipple before taking a quick bite with his front teeth. She showed him how much she liked it by clenching the muscles between her legs and massaging his shaft as she kept up her vertical rhythm.

Now, Lei Mai also started grinding against his shaft using a motion in her hips. The motion looked like a ripple that started in the middle of her torso and wriggled all the way down until it reached her hips. Then, the rippling motion would travel up from her hips and go all the way up her spine, ending with her tossing her head back and letting out a quiet sigh.

Harden was about to explode when he felt her perform those movements on top of him. He let his head fall back against the tub and enjoyed the way she rode him. One of his hands rested on her hip while the other went down to cup the tight little curve of her backside.

Lei Mai leaned back as well. In fact, she let her upper body fall completely back until it appeared as though she was floating on top of the water. Reaching back with both hands, she grabbed hold of the end of the tub opposite of where Harden was resting his head. She grabbed on tightly and spread her legs as far as she could before starting another serpentine dance that caused Harden's eyes to roll up into his skull.

Using all the muscles in her stomach, legs and arms, Lei Mai wriggled her body and worked his as well. She slid herself up and down along his cock so that he could pleasure her without having to lift a finger. The pleasure wasn't one-sided, however.

Far from it.

Harden's entire body stiffened before he exploded inside of her. His hands closed around the sides of the tub with such intensity that he damn near tore off two pieces from the porcelain structure. His climax reached its peak and kept going, even past the point where he thought he could bear the sensations that washed through him.

Lei Mai could feel his body starting to squirm as she kept sliding back and forth. She didn't stop until she managed to get him rubbing against the spot that she wanted, which quickly gave her an orgasm of her own. Her body tensed and she pulled herself up against the side of the tub opposite of Harden. Only when her climax had subsided did she release her grip on him and allow herself to float away.

Harden reached down to retrieve his cigar from the floor. "You see, China doll," he said. "I'll bet I'm the only one that can get you to squeal like that."

"Yes," she said with the slightest hint of sarcasm. "You're the best."

TEN

Clint and Motega had been moving all day. It didn't take long for them to fall into a comfortable rut where they didn't even have to talk constantly to break the silence. Occasionally, they went for an hour or so without a word passing between them, and Clint allowed himself to sit back and enjoy the peace.

It wasn't often that Clint could describe someone as being truly tranquil, but that was the best word to suit the Indian. Normally, a man had to have more years under his belt to find true tranquillity. Even then, it was a rare thing to find someone who was truly at home in silence.

Motega merely walked beside Eclipse and stared up at the sky or at the ground beneath his feet. He seemed completely at ease, even though it hadn't been too long ago that he was running for his life.

Being that it was the thick of winter, the sun was dropping below the horizon fairly early. And both men were ready to stop. The trail passed through a stretch of fairly open country with mountains in the distance and trees scattered all around. It wasn't hard to find a suitable camping spot and even less difficult to gather up enough wood to feed a fire until morning.

By the time the last of the sun's rays were gone and the stars were shimmering in the sky, Clint had gotten a good-sized fire going and was digging through his saddle-bags for some cooking supplies.

"You've got to be ready to keel over," Clint said.

Motega reached around to a small pouch hanging from his belt and removed a scrap of jerky which he clenched between his teeth like a cigarette. "Do I look sick?" he asked with genuine concern.

"No, but even I'm kind of worn out and I did all of my traveling on a horse's back. I feel even more beat just thinking about how you must feel. Do you walk every-where you go?"

"Yes."

"But some of the best riders I've ever seen were Indi-ans. Did you spend too much time learning to fight and not enough time learning to ride?"

Motega grinned and gnawed on the stick of venison in his mouth. "I rode from one end of the world to another when I was younger. At least, that's how it felt back then."

"What happened?" Clint asked, finally feeling as though he might get Motega to say something apart from the casual nonsense he'd said the few times he'd spoken at all throughout the day. "Did you fall off? You know, there's an old saying that if you fall off a horse, you need to get right back on it again."

"That's a saying that came from my people, I think. Just another thing that the white man stole from us."

Clint could tell that Motega wasn't truly going on the defensive, but was merely trying to change the subject. "Seriously, Motega. What happened?"

"Why do you want to know so badly?"

"I don't know. Isn't it customary to kick back and talk around a campfire?"

"I prefer to eat and rest."

"Well, all I've got to eat are some beans and a few strips of bacon, and since that's all I've been eating for the last few days, I wouldn't mind taking my mind off of it. So just answer my question before I force you to drink some of the month-old coffee I'm about to brew."

"All right, Clint," Motega said as he stood and walked to a nearby tree. Crouching down next to the roots, he began pulling up clumps of plants and what looked like grass and weeds. "If I must tell you, then I will." He continued gathering bits and pieces of plants, sniffing them before discarding some and keeping others.

"I was taught to ride by my father. My mother had been taken away from us by soldiers and it saddened me to think of her. So I was taught to become one with the Spirit Mother that resides in the earth and all her creatures.

"I thought it was just a part of my learning to become a man, but my father was teaching me to become a warrior. Besides riding, he taught me to hunt with the blade and spear." Grinning slightly, he walked back over to the campfire and sifted once more through the plants he'd kept. "He taught me to hunt with a bow, but I never could put an arrow into anything that was smaller than a buffalo."

"That's not too bad for a kid," Clint offered.

"Not bad at all, just as long as that buffalo wasn't moving and let me get up to about two or three paces from it. If not, I would miss even that so badly that even my father couldn't find some of the arrows I set loose."

Clint tried to hold back the laugh that tickled the back of his throat, but he couldn't keep all of it from showing on his face. That didn't matter, though, since Motega laughed a bit at his own expense.

"But on the last day my father tried to teach me to use a bow, someone did find the arrow that I'd set loose. He was a man who'd come to this country from the lands far to the east of our ocean. His name was Xiang Po and he set my life on a course that would change it forever."

ELEVEN

When Clint had heard Motega mention a land far to the east, his first thought was Oklahoma or maybe even New York. But when he heard the name Xiang Po, he realized the Indian was talking about something much farther east than New York.

"Zang Poe?" Clint said, doing his best to get the pronunciation right.

"You speak his name as though you might have known him."

"No, but I've met enough Chinese to at least get their names close to sounding right."

Motega's eyes brightened for a moment, but then he nodded and looked back down to the plants he was tearing up and placing into a small pile. "Xiang Po was a wanderer who'd escaped from a company laying railroad tracks into California. His face was scarred and his body was beaten, but he walked with his head high, much like one of my own people's warriors.

"My father told me to respect such a man, even though he didn't know him himself. He said he could see the strength buried inside of the man with the yellowed skin and that such strength was always to be revered."

"Your father sounds like a wise man," Clint said.

"He was. He let Xiang Po share our food and shelter, since he was trying to flee the white man." Motega glanced up at Clint apologetically. "He hated the whites, as do many of my people. I hope you know that I don't mean to—"

"That's all right," Clint interrupted. "No offense taken. Go on with what you were saying."

With a smooth gesture, Motega reached out and plucked the coffeepot from Clint's hand just before he set it over the flames. The Indian held out his other hand and sprinkled the shredded leaves and roots that he'd collected into the coffee grounds. "Don't worry," he said in response to Clint's questioning stare. "This will make the coffee taste a bit better. At least, it will taste better if it's as bad as you were saying it was."

"I guess we'll find out the hard way." With that, Clint grudgingly set the pot onto the fire and nervously watched the enhanced brew start to heat up.

"My father learned much from this Xiang Po. We both did. He stayed with us long enough to watch the moon make its way through its many forms. One of the things he taught me was the one thing my father could not."

"How to hit the broad side of a barn?"

"Yes," Motega answered with a smile. "But not in a way that any of my people would have thought."

"How do you mean?"

Motega reached over his shoulder to pull something from a thin, flat pouch strapped to his back. The pouch was so thin that it conformed to the curve between his shoulder blades and had escaped Clint's notice until that very moment. From that pouch, Motega produced a single arrow. Its tip was made from chipped stone and was similar to any other arrow carried by tribal hunters and warriors.

But Motega didn't hold that arrow as if he was going

to nock it. In fact, he didn't even have a bow.

Gripping the arrow so that its nocked end was resting against his palm and the feathers were between his fingers, Motega cocked his arm back so that the arrow brushed against the back of his neck. From there, he twisted his upper body and snapped his arm out straight, letting the arrow fly from his opened fingers.

Clint reflexively moved back and felt the impulse to reach for his gun simply because the other man had moved so quickly. The arrow hissed through the air like a bullet, its sharpened tip driving into the same tree where Motega had gathered his plants. Even in the flickering light of the campfire, Clint could see that the arrow was buried more than halfway into the thick trunk. Its feathered end was still trembling from the impact.

"Good lord!" Clint said with wide eyes and genuine admiration in his voice. "I've seen some fancy knife throwing and some damn good arrow shooting, but I don't think I've ever seen anything quite like that."

"Neither had my father. Xiang Po started teaching me how to do that just before he left. I showed such a talent for the skill that I earned a new name to carry through manhood. It is the one I carry proudly to this day."

"Really. And what does it mean?"

"Motega means 'new arrow' in the tongue of my father's people. He said I earned it because no arrow could be seen the same after I'd taught it a different way to fly."

"That's impressive."

"It wasn't right away. It took years for me to throw with the power I have today. Much happened in that time and many tears were shed."

"So what happened once this Xiang Po left?" Clint asked. "Did you stop riding as a way to honor him?"

"No. I rode all through my early years and even when I was truly taking on the mantle of a man. I rode out to find Xiang Po so he could complete my teachings and

show me more of his strange ways. I left my father behind
when I should have stayed." Motega's eyes took on a
faraway quality and he stared into the flames. "Even
though he allowed me to go, I should have stayed."

"It sounds like your father was a strong man. He probably wanted you to become strong, too. I don't know the
ways of all the tribes, but don't some of them send off
their young for a while to learn to survive on their own?"

"They do. And this was what my father said as I was
leaving. He told me I would return someday as a true
warrior, even if our paths did not cross again for many
years."

"So did it take that long?"

"I found Xiang Po in a few days. Two moons later, I
went back to search for my father. I rode back to the river
where we lived and found him resting against a stone."
As he spoke, Motega now moved his fingertips through
the fire, letting them stay a bit longer with every pass.
"He'd been shot. There was only one hole in the middle
of his head. His eyes were closed and his hands were
folded on his chest. He must have been sleeping when he
was killed. There was too much fire in his heart for him
to die so easily unless his killers had snuck up on him in
the night."

Clint's first instinct was to tell Motega he was sorry. It
was the customary response to hearing something like
that, but it always seemed so inadequate. This time, it
seemed even more so.

"I picked him up," Motega continued, still gazing into
the fire. "Then I saw that the back of his scalp had been
torn from his head. The tracks were at least a few weeks
old. If I hadn't gone, or even if I'd waited just a little
longer, I would have been there to wake him."

"It doesn't do any good to think like that," Clint said.
"Things happen for a reason, and dwelling on it won't
change anything." But Clint could tell that Motega wasn't

listening. In his mind, the Indian was back at that river on that horrible day.

"I was always a light sleeper," Motega said, waving his hand in and out of the fire. "Now more than ever. I could have woken my father and we could have protected ourselves."

Finally, Motega left his hand in the flames long enough to send a jolt of pain through his arm, which snapped him out of his daze. He looked up at Clint and straightened his back to a proud, rigid posture. "Since he loved his freedom and cherished the Spirit Mother's creatures, I tied my father to his horse and let it carry him away. After that, I could never ride again."

TWELVE

Padre's Crossing wasn't a very big town, but it was still large enough to be divided into many sections. Each of those sections was small, yet very different from the others. The section that Max Emery kept to was the cluster of buildings that had been built by the Chinese who'd come to America to work on the railroads.

Those Chinamen and their families were as much a part of the town as the streets themselves. They made a prosperous living working as merchants and business owners, building up the town just as they'd built up the railroad which now stretched from one end of the country to another.

Max was just about to leave the Chinese section of town when he stopped and turned down an alley which led to a small, secluded lot. The lot appeared to be deserted until he stepped all the way into it. Only then could Max see the narrow building which was as long as a house, yet less than half as wide. For a building so small and in such an out-of-the-way place, there was an awful lot of activity inside and people walking in and out.

Max was used to that and dodged the people leaving the shack as they stumbled toward him as though they didn't even know he was there. As he got closer to the small, coffin-sized door, he took one last breath of fresh air and stepped inside.

The interior of the shack was decorated in plush carpets and large pillows. The air was filled with thick, sweet-smelling smoke, and the only lighting inside was a few candles sputtering in holders here and there. Stepping around a few locals reclining against the wall, Max walked up to an elderly Chinese woman.

"I need to speak to Abe. Is he here?" Max asked, knowing he'd be better off asking than trying to squint through the smoky dark and step over the people laying in a cramped row. "He's tall and has—"

"I know how he looks," the woman interrupted. Pointing toward the middle of the row of people, she said, "He right over there. Been here not too long, yet."

"Good." Now that he knew where to look, Max could pick out the figure he'd been seeking and walked over to where Abe was laying.

Even though he hadn't paid for the privilege as all the others in the shack had, Max was beginning to feel light-headed from just breathing in the smoke, which reeked of opium. The drug was laced with various other spices as well to change its flavor, but it all boiled down to the same thing.

As he passed them, Max saw the other people laying on the carpets and pillows looking up at him. They watched him as if they weren't sure if he was real or a dream. Some looked frightened and others looked amused, but none of them looked up for long before nodding off into whatever visions the opium was giving them.

"Come on, Abe," Max said, kicking at the man laying directly in front of him. "Time to get up and go to work."

Before Max could jab him again with the toe of his boot, Abe sat bolt upright and grabbed hold of the man's foot. "Back the fuck away from me," he snarled, shoving

Max's foot to one side. "I haven't even had a chance for the smoke to kick in yet."

"There's time for that later. Mr. Harden has a job for you."

Although he didn't seem too happy about it, Abe pulled himself up off the floor and onto his feet. He followed Max out of the narrow parlor and tossed a coin into the old Chinese woman's hand. "Keep my spot warm," he told her. After that, he stepped outside and walked over to where Max was waiting.

Standing at well over six feet tall, Abe had the solid build of someone who'd fought to get everything he called his own. His shoulders were wide and his torso was heavy with muscle and sinew. Large, callused hands clenched into fists as he walked, only to unclench moments later.

Abe's head was large and covered in thick red hair. His face was somewhat doughy, and even in the darkness, his eyes were clenched into a tight, suspicious squint. When he walked, he resembled a predator stalking helpless prey.

"You're a damn fool if you think any good is going to come out of that," Max said, jabbing a finger toward the opium den.

Abe looked back to where Max was pointing and shrugged. "Well, I don't think this job you're offering me is gonna be any better for my health."

"That depends on how well you do it. If you're sober enough, you need to head out and see if you can find Jake and the other men he took with him."

"They still haven't brought in that redskin?"

"No. And we haven't even gotten word from them yet."

"Jake usually checks in regular, don't he?"

"Yes, he does. That's why we think something's probably wrong. It could be nothing. He might just be out too far to send someone back, but you need to go and see for sure."

"And what if something did happen to them?"

"Then you get to pick up where they left off." Max's nose wrinkled as he caught a whiff of Abe's clothes. The other man wore a rumpled shirt under a battered vest beneath a leather jacket that was so old that it looked as though it had been pulled inside out. Every bit of the clothing stank of opium, alcohol and worse. Max felt his stomach churn just thinking about it.

"Look, if you can't remember why you were hired, I can remind you," he said. "But you'd be just as well off if you did what you were told and didn't bother yourself with questions. And before you ask, if that Indian is still alive, you can kill him yourself, just try not to mess it up."

Abe shook his head and ran his tongue over the crooked row of his front teeth. He could still taste the little bit of smoke he'd inhaled and tried to savor as much of that as he could before reaching out to take hold of Max by the front of his shirt. Pulling the other man forward with so much force that he nearly took Max off his feet, Abe shoved his face right up to within an inch of Max's.

"You talk to me like I'm some goddamn kid," Abe snarled. His voice didn't slur in the least. In fact, there was enough raw power in it to make it seem as though he'd burned through whatever the opium had given him. "I don't like when you talk to me like that."

All of the superiority Max had felt suddenly disappeared. He was on Abe's turf now and he knew it. "Fine. All right. You made your point."

"I don't think so, Max." One of Abe's beefy hands closed around Max's throat, squeezing just enough to restrict the air headed for his lungs. "You always act like you're better than me just because you get to talk to Harden directly while he sits up there with his painted Chinese whores. Well, I fuck them same whores, Max. And I'll fuck you, too, if you don't start treating me with some goddamn respect."

At that moment, Max felt his heart pounding in his chest and his lungs shrinking within his rib cage. When he tried to pull in a breath, Abe just cut it off, until Max's vision started to fade and the world began to spin around him.

"You hear me?" Abe asked, shaking Max like a doll.

"Y . . . ye . . ." was all Max could manage. Without the ability to speak and with his consciousness quickly leaving him, Max used every bit of his remaining strength to perform one weak nod.

Abe saw the nod and returned it. "There you go," he said, releasing Max's throat, but still holding on to him so he wouldn't collapse. "Now, I think I made my point."

THIRTEEN

Surprisingly enough, the roots and weeds that Motega had prepared did make the coffee taste somewhat more appealing. In fact, after downing half a cup, Clint thought the brew was some of the better coffee he'd had in some time. There was a bit of a muddy aftertaste, but that still beat the hell out of what the stale grounds had tasted like before.

He and the Indian ate their food and swapped a few more stories which were back to the conversational kind of jokes and anecdotes. Clint rested against a tree and wondered if the Indian was going to sleep or if he was just going to sit next to the fire all night. Soon, he noticed that Motega's eyes weren't moving even though the lids weren't quite closed. That was the closest thing that passed for sleep in the Indian's mind, so Clint left him to it so he could get some rest of his own.

In the morning, Clint awoke to the sound of footsteps crunching over snow and dead leaves. He sat up to find Motega pulling the arrow from where he'd driven it into the nearby tree.

"I was going to make some more coffee," Motega said

without so much as glancing back toward Clint. "We should probably get going."

Getting up and stretching his limbs, Clint pulled in a lungful of crisp morning air. Although the breath chilled him all the way down to the soles of his boots, it woke him up and filled him with the clean scent of trees. "I could use some coffee, but we might want to get moving. Those men that were after you probably won't take their time trying to track us down and we didn't exactly go too far in covering our tracks."

"I know. That is how I wanted it. I'm tired of running from them. It's time this was finished once and for all."

"So exactly how long have you been tussling with these fellows?" Clint asked. "You make it sound like there's a lot of history between you."

Motega nodded and spun the arrow in one hand quickly enough to make a whirling, whistling sound of the tip cutting through the air. "These men are responsible for the pain of someone dear to me."

"Did they hurt your father?"

"Not my father," Motega said, bringing the arrow to a sudden stop by closing his fist around its middle. "My master."

"Master? What do you mean?" The only time Clint had heard someone refer to another as his master, it was a slave talking about his owner. The very concept of slavery was an insult in Clint's mind, and he hated the thought of offending Motega by bringing it up. Still, it was difficult for him to wait for the Indian to find the right words he wanted to say.

After putting the arrow back into its place on his back, Motega busied himself with the familiar ritual of preparing the roots and leaves for the coffee that was to come. "After my father died, I had nowhere else to go. I had no home, and even the shelter offered by my own people didn't feel comforting to me. So I sought out the only direction I had in life, which was the direction offered by Xiang Po.

"He took me in as though I was his only son and taught me all of his ways. And since I had the rest of my life to learn from him, he started me down the path that he still walked. In his language, it was called karate. In ours, it means 'empty hand,' and it was the way of the empty hand that allowed me to see beyond my father's death into something bigger."

"I've heard of karate from a few men I knew in San Francisco," Clint said. "I even saw one man lay out a drunk twice his size in under a second, but it didn't look like what you did yesterday."

"Master Po began learning karate and added styles from every other land he visited. That's why he wandered this land, so he could study and apply what he saw in his own way. He taught me more than any white man could learn in their schools.

"He taught me to read and speak in many tongues. He even taught me to become more at peace with the Great Spirit and our Mother Earth. I owe all that I am to Master Po, just as I do my father."

"So what happened to him?"

"He was offered a job by a man in the town we'll reach today. It was not the kind of job Master Po would ever consider, and he told that to the man who'd offered it to him. The other man responded with force at first, but that was not nearly enough to persuade Master Po."

Clint let out a quick laugh. "If this Po was the one who taught you how to fight, I bet he made his point pretty damn well."

"You could say that," Motega said with a little smirk of his own. "In my years of learning, I was only ever to get the upper hand on him once. And even that didn't last more than a second." The Indian's lighter mood lasted about that long as well, and he was quickly drawn back into the present.

"My master roamed this land and many others for most of his life, but he was still considered an indentured servant since that was how he was brought to this country. That was how this other man finally beat him. Not with guns or in any kind of fight," Motega said with a burning contempt in his eyes. "But with an unfair law meant to keep a free spirit enslaved. A law especially suited to the white man."

Once again, Clint felt the need to defend himself simply because he was in the same race that Motega was insulting. But he couldn't do that too well knowing what he knew about how the Indians and Chinese had been treated. So he kept quiet and allowed the Indian to finish his tale.

"This man's name is Albert Harden," Motega said after a moment or two of silence. "I learned this from the last message left to me from my master. He told me this man's name and where he lived. That was all he could tell me since that was all he knew.

"This Albert Harden holds the contract that serves to bind my master's life and he will use that to get Master Po to perform this job. If he does not, I fear my master will be killed."

"Surely your master could get away from these men," Clint said. "It doesn't sound like he's exactly the helpless type."

Motega shook his head. "He will fight, but he will not run. I know only too well that once a white man has his laws behind him, he becomes much more powerful. Besides, do you truly think any sheriff or deputy will think twice before bringing in an old Chinese man on the orders of a rich landowner?"

Clint didn't even really have to think about that one.

As much as it galled him to admit it, he said, "No. Probably not."

"That is why I must find him myself."

"And what then? Kill this Harden fellow? If he's after your master, then he's probably the kind of man to have hired guns working for him. Are you prepared to fight them, too? Are you prepared to kill those men to get to where you want to go?"

"That is the choice Harden made when he started this."

"And it's your choice to finish it."

Fixing his eyes onto Clint, Motega stared at him for a few tense moments before saying, "Are you going to try and stop me, Clint?"

"Only if you plan on becoming a murderer. If that's the case, I'll step in just as quickly as I did when I saw those men trying to kill you."

"I'm sure my father's people would have me kill you for trying to get in the way of me trying to help my loved one. A warrior would not stand to be threatened when he is taking on such an important task." Pausing for a few moments, Motega nodded slowly and let some of the tension drain from his muscles. "But my master would see things differently. He would say you are an honorable man and are acting in the best way you know."

"So which are you going to listen to?" Clint asked. Although he didn't move for his pistol, Clint was ready to draw the Colt at any time.

"I don't believe you are truly going to stand in my way, Clint. Therefore, both of my families would be ashamed if I tried to hurt you."

"I'm glad to hear you say that, because I've got a few ideas on how to work with this Harden without going straight for the throat."

"And if blood must be spilled?"

"Let's just cross that bridge when we get to it."

FOURTEEN

After a quick breakfast and a shared pot of coffee, Clint and Motega were back on the trail and headed for Padre's Crossing. All the while, they had been keeping their eyes and ears open for any sign that they were being followed, but they saw and heard nothing. As far as they could tell, the four riflemen had decided against another ambush, but neither Clint nor Motega thought that the gunmen had given up entirely.

Even though the Indian still insisted on walking next to Clint and Eclipse, they made much better time this day than they had before. It was as though Motega was drawing energy from being so close to his goal and using that to fuel the fire inside him that kept him moving.

Clint could feel the rush of his blood as well. It pumped through his body and got his mind racing in new directions. After they'd been on the move for a few hours, he began talking through some strategy for when they arrived in town. Although he hadn't heard of Albert Harden, he figured it was best to assume that this was more than just some tough-talking bully.

What grieved Clint more and more the longer he thought about it was the simple fact that Motega had been right. A white man with any kind of standing would automatically be supported over any Indian or Chinese. There were a few exceptions, of course, but those were very few and far between. So since changing the country's state of mind was well out of his reach, Clint decided to use it to his advantage. In this case, it should work out to Motega's advantage as well.

He discussed this with the Indian as they made their way toward Padre's Crossing. As they spoke and planned, the day slipped away from them even faster than they could believe. After what seemed like only a few hours, the town could be spotted in the distance and the trail straightened out to head right for it.

"We should be there well before sundown," Clint said, shielding his eyes from the light with an upraised hand. "There might even be some time to get something to eat before we start in on rattling Harden's cage."

"I would have preferred to start rattling even sooner," Motega replied. "But I have had to slow myself down to accommodate your leisurely pace."

"Oh, what's this now? After two days, you finally sprout a sense of humor? If you'd like to settle this with a race, then by all means just let me know."

"If that is the only way to speed your steps, then I would be happy to oblige you."

Clint was looking down at the Indian, smirking at the way Motega kept his face relatively passive. No matter what the other man said, it was downright difficult for Clint to figure out whether or not Motega was kidding. Finally, Clint dismissed the boastful talk with a quick wave. "You'd better save your strength. Once we get to town, we're going to need it."

"So you don't wish to race?" Motega asked with a trace of disappointment. "And I thought we could trim some time off our journey after all."

"Just trying to save you some embarrassment," Clint

said. "But if you'd really like to go for it, then let's get going. I'm sure Eclipse could use a little run to clear his head."

Motega looked over to the Darley Arabian's eyes and reached out to place one hand along the stallion's face. While looking at the horse, he stroked Eclipse's ear as well as the side of his head. "I believe you're right, Clint. He does look anxious. It seems even he is tired of slowing to your ambling crawl."

Straightening up in the saddle, Clint pulled the reins to put some distance between himself and the Indian. "All right, that's it. You want a race? Then you got it. On three. One . . . two . . . three!"

After signaling for the race to begin, Clint snapped his reins and hunkered down in preparation for Eclipse's burst of speed. Beside him, Motega had already sprung forward like an arrow that had been loosed from the bow.

The Indian held his body down close to the ground, his legs pumping furiously beneath him in quick, stabbing lines that threw him forward. He held his arms out in front of him, but kept them relatively still. Rather than flail them at his sides the way most people ran, he kept his elbows tucked against his ribs and his hands held slightly out as if to catch him should he lose his footing.

Watching Motega from the saddle, Clint admired the other man's speed, but wondered how he expected to out-run a horse. The next thing Clint wondered was why Motega was so far ahead of him.

FIFTEEN

Clint saw that he was indeed moving. Eclipse was trotting at a lively pace, but wasn't anywhere close to breaking into a run. The Darley Arabian let out huffing breaths as though he was straining against a rope that was holding him back. As he began to snort loudly, the stallion bobbed his head up and down before shaking it from side to side.

Clint gave the reins another snap, but all that did was make Eclipse fret more and let out a few more angry snorts. "Come on, boy," he urged, lightly touching his heels to Eclipse's sides. "What's the matter with you?"

Clint could feel the tension building up in the horse's muscles and he could hear the strain in Eclipse's breath. After a few more seconds, the stallion began picking up speed, until he finally launched himself into an awkward run.

Now that he was moving faster, Clint looked up to find Motega. At that same instant, the Indian looked over his shoulder back at him. Of course, Motega was looking back from a distance of close to a hundred yards up the trail.

Motega stood in his statue-like stance with his arms folded across his chest and waited for Eclipse to finally bring Clint to him. Once the horse and rider had come to a stop, Motega reached out with his hand and once again began stroking the side of Eclipse's face.

As soon as he could, Clint swung down from the saddle and walked around to get a look at Eclipse's face. "What the hell happened back there?" he asked while examining the stallion for himself.

Keeping his fingers pressed against the Darley Arabian's temple, Motega massaged a small circle which slowly widened. Eclipse leaned in closer to the Indian as though he was afraid Motega might take his hand away.

"Don't worry about your four-legged companion," Motega said. "I would never want to harm such a fine creature as this."

Watching the way Motega was working his fingers, Clint picked up on the fact that he wasn't just petting Eclipse's head. In fact, he'd been doing more than that before the race as well. "What did you do to him, Motega?"

"Nothing that I can't fix right about . . . now."

As he said that, Motega pressed his fingertip into a small groove between Eclipse's temple and ear. He pressed in the tip of one finger and twisted slightly, until the stallion let out a breath that had been building up in the back of his throat.

Just as Clint was about to pull Motega's hand away, he noticed that all the tension had left Eclipse's body and the stallion even seemed to be nuzzling the Indian affectionately.

"One more time," Clint said with quickly fading patience. "What did you do to him?"

"Just a simple trick taught to me by my master. There are pressure points in every living thing's body, whether you are horse or man. Some of those points can cause pain and others pleasure. Some can even kill, while others simply make you too weary to run." When he said that last part, Motega looked over to Clint with a sly grin.

"This animal has a powerful spirit," Motega said. "I've never seen one break through that technique so quickly. I'd say he would have been up to full speed in another second or two. You should be proud."

Clint ran his hands over Eclipse's neck and face and said, "You're sure nothing's wrong with him?"

"See for yourself."

It wasn't long before Clint was satisfied the Darley Arabian was back to normal. In fact, Eclipse seemed even more rested than he had after a night's sleep. "You sure take your races seriously, Motega."

"Master Po once told me that cockiness will do more damage to a man than any other sin and may even lead him to his death. You had that cockiness written on your face back there, friend. All I did was wipe it off."

"Yeah, well, I guess I had it coming." Now that he saw Eclipse moving and breathing normally again, Clint relaxed quite a bit himself. "That was one hell of a trick. I'll bet it comes in pretty useful."

"Well, another thing Master Po said was that if I insisted on walking, I must be ready to deal with those who aren't so ambitious."

Clint decided to lead Eclipse by the reins the rest of the way into town. He couldn't quite keep up with Motega, but he went a hell of a lot faster than he might have guessed. Although he still wasn't sure if the two of them could get to Master Po, he knew Albert Harden was in for one hell of a fight.

SIXTEEN

Abe had ridden straight through most of the last day and a half without stopping for more than a quick rest here and there. He could tell his horse was getting exhausted, but that was hardly any concern of his. He figured that didn't become his problem until it seemed that the animal might drop over before delivering him to where he wanted to go. As far as he could tell, Abe guessed he could go another half day before that happened.

Pushing that to the back of his mind, Abe dug his spurs into the horse's ribs and let out a powerful holler to put some extra steam into the beast's strides. Despite the aching in its belly and the foam dripping from its mouth, the horse did its best to oblige the command and thundered farther away from the trail, which had been left behind at the start.

Abe knew where Jake Riley and the others were headed because he'd been the one to tell the riflemen where to start looking for the Indian that had gotten away. For the rest of the time, he'd stewed while the others were sent off to actually bring in the redskin, while he had to stay in town. He could have always gone off on his own, and had considered that on more than one occasion. But in the end, it always boiled down to money. If Harden didn't like what Abe did, odds were good that Abe wouldn't see any more of that man's money.

So Abe had drowned the knot in his gut with booze, and even tried to suffocate it in opium smoke. Both of those were fairly effective methods, but weren't enough to get at the root of what was truly bothering the bulky redheaded man.

What really got to him was the fact that both the Chinaman and the redskin were still alive. More than that, the Chinaman had a knack for smiling at him every time Abe had gone to try and get under the old man's yellow hide. Just thinking about it had damn near whipped Abe into a killing frenzy, and the only thing saving the Chinaman's life was Harden's standing order to keep him breathing.

Abe thought of himself as a man who did whatever the hell he wanted whenever he wanted to do it, which made this job all the more difficult to bear. That knot in his stomach had only twisted around inside of him, growing every second that passed where Abe felt that he was at the end of someone else's leash.

That feeling was nowhere to be found, however, now that Abe was on his horse and had put Padre's Crossing behind him. He enjoyed racing over the landscape so much that he almost forgot what he was racing for. It was easy to get sidetracked with a few days' worth of whiskey and pungent smoke still burning through his system. All he had to do was think about that Chinaman's grinning face, however, and Abe was pulled right back in the right direction.

Killing that Indian would go a long way toward getting rid of that smile for good. Abe had a knack for sniffing out another man's weaknesses, and he could tell that the Chinaman had a soft spot for that redskin. Although he didn't know why that soft spot was there, Abe didn't waste too much time trying to figure it out.

All he needed to know was where he could most hurt another man. After that, all he needed to do was sit back and listen to the screams.

There wasn't much farther to go before Abe reached the spot where he thought he might catch up to Jake and the others. The shortcut he'd taken had shaved a good amount of time off the trip, but not enough, considering Riley had such a big head start. Even so, he figured it would be a good idea to ease up a bit before the horse fell over with him on its back.

Abe stopped jabbing his spurs into the same bloody spots on the animal's sides and even refrained from snapping the reins. The horse still kept up a good pace, but that was out of pure fear of getting another beating. Satisfied, Abe let the horse run for its life. There would be time to rest as soon as he caught up with the riflemen.

At that moment, Abe caught sight of something that made him lean suddenly forward and squint into the distance. If it wasn't for the pale, wintry sun, which kept fairly low to the horizon even at the peak of afternoon, the man's eyes might have missed the shapes up ahead. But Abe didn't miss a thing, especially when he was so anxious to spill the redskin's blood that he could almost taste it on his tongue.

He didn't even feel the relentless wind that had taken on such a chill that it sliced through his entire body. He didn't even feel the horse shudder beneath the saddle as the grueling ride caught up to him in a rush of painful fatigue. The only thing Abe paid any attention to was the group of figures laying on the ground about a quarter mile ahead.

The land was flat enough in this part of the country that distances could be fairly difficult to judge. But having grown up in and around the mountains, Abe only needed a second to gauge how far it was between him and those dark spots clustered on the grass between some rocks. He turned his eyes to a spot just past those rocks and immediately spotted another group of shapes that were darker against the backdrop of trees.

Unlike the first group of shapes, those second ones were not only bigger, but they were moving as well. They weren't exactly running from one spot to another, but they were indeed moving slowly back and forth, as if pacing to pass the time.

Abe's eyes were good, but he didn't need to strain them to figure out what that second group of shapes actually were. They made the first ones look small in comparison, and moved about on four legs. Suddenly, Abe cared even less about his horse's health, since he now knew for certain that there were a few others close by to take its place.

Driving the horse as fast as it could go, Abe quickly counted four shapes laying on the ground. Just as he'd figured when he'd first spotted them, they were men sprawled in the grass, and they had yet to make a move that Abe could see.

He watched the horses walking about while he rode on. Try as he might, Abe could only spot three of the bigger shapes milling near their fallen riders. Abe's lips parted into a venomous sneer. Now, on top of everything else, that damn Injun had become a horse thief as well.

SEVENTEEN

By the time Abe got to within ten yards of where the riflemen were laying, he could feel his horse straining for each and every breath. The animal made hard, hacking sounds every time it exhaled and its sides shook as though every one of its innards was trembling.

Although Abe noticed these things, he hardly paid them any mind. Instead, he focused his attention on what was ahead. Before he got close enough to see the fallen men's faces, Abe brought his horse to a stop and dropped down from the saddle. His hand went down to rest on the .44 on his hip and he took on a posture similar to a stalking wolf.

Behind him, Abe's horse slowly lowered itself down so that it could lay on the ground with its legs folded beneath it. The animal struggled to keep air flowing in and out of its nostrils and now had white foam dripping from its mouth.

Abe moved forward, pulling the gun from its holster and holding it so that the barrel was trained on the space directly in front of him. His finger tightened on the trigger, even though the only things he could see that were moving were the horses which grazed on the nearby grass.

After taking a few more steps, Abe stopped and narrowed his eyes until they were dark, intense slits. For the next couple of seconds, he didn't even breathe, as he turned his head from side to side, absorbing every last detail of the area around him. He could hear the horses breathing and chomping on the grass nearby, as well as the animal wheezing desperately behind him. Abe could smell the snow that was set to fall in the next couple of hours and could feel the cold soaking up from the ground through the bottoms of his boots.

Finally, Abe allowed his back to straighten and his gun to lower slightly. After soaking up all he could, the big man was satisfied that there wasn't anything he needed to concern himself with at that particular moment. He holstered the pistol and only shot a quick glance over his shoulder when he heard his horse let out a final, shuddering breath.

No big loss, he figured, as the animal's head slumped to the ground. That one was getting long in the tooth anyway.

Abe walked up to the closest figure on the ground. None of the fallen men had so much as stirred since he'd spotted them. But all Abe had to do was take one sniff of the air to know that all four of them were dead.

Death had a pungent stench all its own and Abe knew it all too well. That particular stench wasn't overpowering since the bodies were laying in the open, but it was there all the same. It hung on the breeze like a stain that soiled a curtain over a window. Abe picked up on the scent without a problem, where many others might have mistaken it for any of nature's other less welcome smells.

Crouching down next to that closest figure, Abe reached out and took hold of it by the shoulder. The figure was laying on its side, so he rolled it onto its back and took a look at its face. Sure enough, the man was one of Jake Riley's boys. In fact, the man's rifle was still gripped

in his hand, which had been hidden beneath the rest of
the body.

Abe made his way around to the rest of the bodies,
looking at each in turn and nodding when he recognized
the features. Jake was the last man he stepped to, and this
was partly because Abe had picked out which of the four
was Jake's body. He saved the best for last and glared
down at Jake's blank, open eyes for a long couple of
seconds.

"You stupid bastard," Abe said, as though any of the
four men were in any condition to listen. "One goddamn
Injun and you can't even kill him without getting yourself
killed instead." Crouching down, Abe began searching
Jake's body with both hands, pulling open the other man's
jacket as he said, "Let's see what happened to you."

Although Abe was a far cry from being any kind of
doctor, he'd delivered enough wounds to other men to be
able to know where to look for them. At first, he went
through the motions of looking over the body and rolling
it back and forth to see front and back. Before too long,
however, he let the body slump back to the ground.

Abe stared down at the corpse with growing confusion.
"What the hell?" he muttered as he searched the dead
figure one more time.

The second time left him just as perplexed as the first,
since neither search had given him any clue as to what
might have done Jake Riley in. There was no blood soaking through his clothes and no wound that Abe could see.
Apart from a few dark bruises on Jake's neck and face,
it seemed as though Riley should have been able to get
up and speak for himself.

Searching the rest of the bodies didn't help matters in
the least. After half an hour had gone by, Abe hadn't been
able to uncover anything more besides a few more bruises
and a few spent rifle casings. Not a complete loss—Abe's
efforts had told him two things.

First of all, Jake and his men had been shooting at something.

And second, whoever had killed the four riflemen had probably used his bare hands.

EIGHTEEN

Clint and Motega made it into Padre's Crossing right when they thought they would. They could have arrived a bit sooner, but they took their time and discussed what they would do when they got there. Together, they came up with a plan that was simple, yet seemed fairly effective. Sometimes, Clint knew, it was best to keep things simple. Not only were there fewer things to go wrong, but it was easier to spot them when they did.

Of course, that was all in theory. Plenty of things seemed better in theory. Clint knew that only too well. The only problem with a plan that involved dealing with dangerous types was that a single mistake could very well cost a man his life.

Those were high stakes indeed, but Clint and Motega agreed that they would sit in on the game anyway. In the back of his mind, Clint made plans of his own just in case the Indian turned out to be something very different than what he appeared to be. So far, Clint felt good about his impressions of the other man, but that wasn't exactly gospel. He'd been wrong before and he would be wrong again. That was all a nasty part of being human.

For the meantime, Clint had committed himself to the

plan that he and Motega had formed. The Indian seemed earnest enough in what he'd told Clint and seemed to genuinely need his help. At the very least, Clint knew that there were gunmen out to put a bullet through Motega's head. That was enough to warrant a helping hand and the benefit of the doubt.

At least, that was enough for the moment.

They entered into the town's limits in the same way they'd been traveling for the last couple days. Clint rode on Eclipse's back and Motega walked beside him. The Indian kept his head down, however, and his shoulders slumped. His eyes still burned with their passionate fire, but they were pointed toward the ground, not even rising to meet the locals who stopped to take in the sight of the two new arrivals.

There was still plenty of suspicion in the people's eyes, however, but that was understandable since Clint was holding on to a rope that was tied around Motega's neck. The Indian's hands were bound at the wrists and his feet were tied together at the ankles. Even with so much constraint, Motega still managed to move smoothly and keep up with Clint as he slowly rode along.

Clint led Motega through the streets without making a fuss. He knew he didn't have to say a word to announce his presence there, since word would spread well enough on its own. That was just fine with the two of them, since making a little scene like this was all a part of their plan. They couldn't afford for the scene to last too long, but it was essential for plenty of folks to witness it while it lasted.

It was obvious what the locals were thinking just by the way they looked at them. Some of them looked a bit afraid of the sight, but mostly they looked at Motega much the way they would stare at an animal on display at a circus. Every now and then, the stares would burn into Motega's skin, causing him to look up for just a sec-

ond at the people on the side of the street. That was all
it took for those people to look away and quickly get back
to their business.

Motega fought to keep his head down for as long as he
could. Normally, he was accustomed to walking proudly
and standing tall. For the sake of the plan, however, he
played the role of frightened prisoner and even acted as
though it was a struggle to keep up with Eclipse.

This time, Clint was the one who had his head held
high, and he met every glance that came his way with a
cordial smile and a tip of his hat. Despite the fact that
they were an unlikely pair, they attracted more than their
fair share of attention as they made their way down the
main street and turned into the business district.

"Where to from here?" Clint asked by whispering out
of the corner of his mouth.

Motega looked up for a second and then dropped his
face back down again. "Turn left at this next corner."

"Thanks."

Clint followed the directions he'd been given until he
saw a definite change in the buildings and locals around
him. The structures were still the same basic size and
shape, but their signs were no longer written in English.
The decorations hanging in the windows or around the
doors were foreign as well, every one of them distinctly
Eastern in appearance.

It didn't take an expert to know that this part of town
was predominantly Chinese. In fact, if he forgot about the
rest of Padre's Crossing and focused on just the street in
front of him, Clint might have been fooled into thinking
that he'd left the mainland altogether.

The writing in the windows was in blocky, oriental
characters, only a few of which had English translations
written close by. The faces around him had shifted as
well, until Clint felt very much like the trespasser amid a
sea of curious narrow eyes and dark black hair.

As odd as it was at first, Clint quickly adjusted to his surroundings and even began soaking up some of the colorful, exotic paintings decorating the storefronts. Even the Chinese locals smiled up to him and greeted him just as the people had in the outer part of town. Clint felt the curious eyes hovering on him, but didn't feel any less welcome.

"There," Motega said with a subtle nod toward a building a bit farther down the street. "Harden will be in that place."

Luckily, the building Motega was talking about was labeled with a large sign in the window that was written in both Chinese and English lettering. It was a large, two-floor building that looked as though it had just been given a fresh coat of creamy white paint with dark green trim.

"You mean the Oriental Palace?" Clint asked, reading what was written on the large building's front window.

"Yes. But before you go there, stop now and drop me off." Motega came to a halt directly in front of a small storefront that was labeled strictly in Chinese lettering. The Oriental Palace was less than half a block up the street. "I should be able to rest here where I won't be in any immediate danger."

"You sure about that?" Clint asked.

"Yes. Walk me inside and continue on. I'll wait here. Trust me. We don't have much time before Harden hears about our arrival and sends someone out to meet us."

Clint dropped down from the saddle, tied Eclipse to a post in front of the small building and led Motega inside.

NINETEEN

Although none of the locals had made any threatening moves toward Clint or the man acting as his prisoner, every one of them was studying them carefully. Clint could feel their curiosity rising with every second, which made it feel that much better to be inside and away from all those inquisitive stares.

Most of the people were the same sort that one would expect to see walking the street toward the end of the day. No matter what their race or heritage, they were simply folks making their way home or to one of the many stores and businesses in the area. They were all ages, and most were friendly enough.

Only a few of them looked at Clint with open hostility, and that was immediately after they'd gotten a look at Motega and the way he was being led like a dog on a leash. Every now and then, Clint wished that the Indian wasn't so good at playing his part as prisoner. That was mainly because it was so contrary to Clint's nature to take on his own part. For the moment, he had to attract attention, and putting up with prying eyes was all a part of it. It still felt good to go into the small building and get away from the glare of all those prying eyes.

Of course, inside the little storefront, they were greeted by a whole new set of prying eyes.

Most of the light in the room came from the door that Clint and Motega had used to enter the place. It promptly vanished when Clint let the door slam shut behind him. There were a few candles scattered on small end tables, as well as a lantern hanging on the closest wall. All of those weren't enough to light the room too well, however, and that gave the place a strange, mysterious feel.

Bits of dust drifted through what little light there was, settling on chipped wooden furniture covered with tattered cloths embroidered with more Chinese letters and pictures. The smell of incense hung in the air as well. It wasn't overpowering, but merely what was leftover from the last time a scented stick had been burned within those walls.

A quick glance was all Clint needed to spot a couple figures standing here and there as well as a few chairs set up against the wall. A hallway was in the back of the room, leading farther inside the building. Judging by the rows of doors in that hallway, Clint guessed the place was a hotel or a cathouse. Since the only thing he could hear was the tinkle of wind chimes and someone clearing his throat, he leaned more toward the hotel idea.

Suddenly, Clint felt very aware of those few eyes drilling into him. They weren't outright threatening yet, but they were not half as cordial as the ones he'd seen outside in the street.

Reminding himself that he wanted to draw some attention his way, Clint tipped his hat to a short man standing behind a battered counter, dressed in a dark blue jacket and matching pants. On top of the counter was a pencil and a large book opened in the middle to display rows of scribbled names. Most of those names were written in English and the rest were in Chinese. All of them, however, told Clint that he was indeed inside a hotel.

"Pleased to meet you, sir," Clint said to the man behind the counter. "I wonder if you—"

"Motega?" the short man behind the counter said. "Could that truly be you?"

The Indian lifted his chin so that his face could be more easily seen. He wore a subtle smile and nodded once to the Chinese man's inquiry.

The Chinese man had a narrow face that was covered with smooth, leathery skin. There were deep creases in his cheeks and near his eyes that resembled miniature versions of canyons crisscrossing a desert. He smiled warmly at Motega, but when he looked over to Clint, his eyes dropped to the rope in his hand that led to Motega's neck.

Clint had just started to return the smile when he noticed that the Chinese man no longer seemed too friendly. In fact, every bit of warmth had disappeared from his eyes, to be replaced by jarring cold. His hand dropped beneath the counter and snapped back up holding a small pistol that was cocked and ready to fire.

Seeing that, Clint reflexively went for his Colt and plucked the gun from its holster, just as he noticed another nasty change in the room. Before, he'd picked out two or three other people standing around in different parts of the dark room. Now there were twice that many, and every last one of them was pointing a gun at Clint's face.

TWENTY

Clint watched Motega, but only out of the corner of his eye. The rest of his attention was divided among the other weapons that were aimed at him from the hands of several irate Chinese. The man behind the counter looked shocked that Clint had not only gone for his gun, but managed to draw the weapon and aim it in the space of a heartbeat.

Glancing around to make sure the others were still backing his play, the man behind the counter found some more courage and brought his gun back up to bear. "You stepped into the wrong place, round eye," he said with only a hint of an accent.

Motega stepped forward and held both arms out to block Clint from the others farther inside the room. He then looked over to the man behind the counter and said, "It's all right, Tam. This isn't as bad as it looks."

The man behind the counter kept his eyes on Clint, but spoke to the Indian. "You're sure you can trust this one?"

"Already, he has saved my life once. For that, I am sure I can trust him. At least, for the moment."

Even with that last bit tacked onto the end of it, Motega's endorsement seemed to carry a lot of weight. It only took a few seconds for the guns to be lowered and

secreted away within holsters and under baggy shirts. The
man behind the counter had yet to lower his gun, however, and he watched Clint with open suspicion.

Sensing that Tam was just being cautious, Clint slowly
lowered his Colt and slid it back into his holster. He then
opened both hands and placed them flat on the counter.

That went a long way, since Tam nodded slowly and
finally hid his own weapon under the counter. "Why you
bring him here?" he asked, still clearly talking to Motega.
"Now if you're wrong about him, I will have to move to
another place. Probably another town."

Motega held up his bound hands and stuck them out
toward Clint. "If I'm wrong about him, you can shoot him
just as easily then as you could a moment ago."

Shaking his head, Clint untied the Indian's restraints
and looped the rope around his shoulder. "You know, this
town seemed pretty friendly when we first rode in. Looks
like I was sure wrong about that."

"Tam is just being a good protector to someone he's
taken under his wing. If not for that, I would not feel safe
staying here so close to the viper's nest."

Once he'd taken the bindings from Motega's wrists,
neck and ankles, Clint sensed an immediate drop in the
hostility within the room. There were only a couple others
to be seen, apart from Tam, but Clint wasn't about to let
himself think that there weren't more hiding in the shadows.

"How much to rent a room?" Clint asked.

Tam looked first at Motega and then to Clint. Finally,
he allowed a faint smile to cross his lips and said, "Our
friends stay free. Everyone else pay fifty cent a day."

"Cheap rates."

"Cheap rooms."

"So do I pay now or later?"

"Keep money for now," Tam answered. "If Motega is

wrong about you after all, you won't walk out of town alive."

"Sounds good to me," Clint said with a broad smile. "At least either way I won't have to pay."

For a moment, Tam and the other Chinese in the place merely stared at Clint as though he'd sprouted a set of bull horns. Then, starting with the man behind the counter, a wave of laughter worked through the room and filled the dimly lit space.

"Round eye has sense of humor," Tam said. "Better than most in this town. You go about your business and come back when you're done. Use the back door so nobody see you come inside. You can rest here. Nobody tells that they even see you walk through this door."

Motega reached down toward the counter and took hold of the book of names. He flipped the register shut with one quick motion and locked his eyes onto Tam's. "Since when has my word not been enough to gain your trust?"

Tam froze for a second and glanced nervously back and forth between the Indian and Clint. "Your word is fine, but he—"

"He is the one I introduced as my friend. That should be more than enough to end this treatment of him."

Nodding, Tam said, "You are right, Motega." He then looked to Clint and bowed slightly at the waist. "My apologies. You are welcome here as guest. Forgive me for being cautious."

"My name's Clint Adams and I'm a firm believer in caution."

"Clint Adams?" Tam asked, his eyebrows perking up. "I have heard this name before."

"Then you probably don't believe me about the cautious part."

"From what I hear, you are a man who will walk through fire for the proper cause. Again, you have my sincere and humble apology." Tam bowed again, lower this time, while pressing his palms flat against each other in front of him. "Consider this dwelling your own."

Although it was nice to feel welcomed, Clint was beginning to get a little uncomfortable with the drastic way the pendulum had swung. Only seconds ago, he'd been staring down the barrels of guns and now he felt like a returning hero.

"No need for all of that," Clint said. As he turned around, he saw that the other people in the room were bowing as well. "Really. Your apology's accepted."

Tam and the others lifted their heads, and all the tension in the room faded away. "When you return," Tam said, "take the last room in the hall. That will be the first since you must not forget to—"

"I know," Clint cut in. "I've got to use the back door. Got it."

Once again, Tam bowed and sat back down behind the counter.

Motega faced Clint and lifted his hand in farewell before turning and heading down the hall. The Indian seemed to disappear into the quiet shadows before he even got close to the first numbered door.

TWENTY-ONE

Albert Harden was dressed in a pearl gray suit made out of perfectly tailored silk. Every angle of the garment fit him so precisely that it seemed as though the material had been stitched together after he was already inside it. A silver watch chain hung across his waist, and he removed the timepiece to press the little button on top.

"Where the hell is that man?" he grumbled after taking a quick glance at the watch's mother-of-pearl face.

He stood in a room at the front of the second floor of the Oriental Palace. It was the suite directly across the hall from the one where he frequently bathed with his favorite China doll. The room he currently occupied was filled with all the light the day had left to offer. Although it was enough to illuminate the space, it wasn't enough to do much more than that. The sun was dropping quickly, obscured behind a thick bank of clouds.

A picture window took up a good portion of the room's back wall. It was at that window that Harden stood with one hand propped on his hip and the other grasping the expensive timepiece. Behind him, Max Emery stood like an attentive puppy and a brunette in her late twenties sat reclining in a padded chaise lounge.

When he reached down to slide the watch back into its
little pocket, Harden pulled open his waistcoat just enough
to reveal the edge of a black leather shoulder holster. That
little glimpse was the only visible clue that the holster
was even there. As soon as Harden pulled the coat closed
again, it fell over the holster so perfectly that not so much
as a bulge remained.

"Have you heard anything from him, Max?" Harden
asked.

The younger man shook his head even though Harden
still had his back to him and was looking out the window.
"Not yet. But you know how Abe works. He'll be back
whenever he gets here, but he should at least have some
results."

"Yeah. So far, those results are the only things keeping
me from letting the law have his sorry ass. Lord knows
the sheriff's been after me to turn Abe over ever since I
put him on the payroll."

"Well, that still might not be such a bad id—"

Max was cut off in mid-sentence as the door suddenly
burst open and a young girl in her late teens flew into the
room. She went straight to the brunette laying on the
chaise lounge and stopped short when she saw the angry
glare that Max was throwing at her.

Max pulled in a breath and puffed out his chest. He
took one step toward the young girl before he was stopped
by the brunette who'd jumped off the chaise lounge and
dashed to put herself in front of the girl.

"Don't worry, you've scared her plenty," the brunette
said. "I'm sure you're real proud of yourself now."

"This room is supposed to be off limits, Elle," Max
said to the brunette. "We can't have these whores running
in here whenever they feel like it."

Hearing that, the brunette straightened up, cocked her
hand back and cut loose with a vicious slap that filled the
room with a loud noise of flesh on flesh. The impact was

powerful enough to snap Max's head all the way in one direction.

When he turned back to face her, Max's eyes were angry enough to melt steel.

"She is not a whore," Elle said, standing her ground even when it looked like she was going to get her slap returned with interest.

Max lifted his hand and balled it into a fist, drawing it back slowly for maximum effect.

"Best think twice, Max," Harden said. He was still standing at the window and was watching the confrontation with mild interest. He wasn't involved enough to turn completely around, however, and was looking over his shoulder at the trio. "You hit her too hard and she won't stop nagging till I take it out on you. It might be less painful to apologize."

He had to think about it for a moment or two, but eventually Max relaxed his fist and lowered his arm. "Sorry, Elle." Turning toward the young girl, he said, "Sorry to you also."

The girl looked as though she didn't know exactly how to react. When she got a nod from Elle, she curtsied once and then looked back to the brunette. "I was supposed to come tell you something. Miss Lin told me to come here as quick as I could so I could tell you."

Miss Lin was the owner of the Oriental Palace, and everyone in the room recognized the name. "Then go ahead and tell me," Elle said soothingly. "Don't be afraid."

"A stranger just rode into town," the girl said quickly. "He was dragging some other man along with him. Had him tied with a rope around his neck like he was gonna hang him."

Max was already losing what little patience he had. "What are you talking about?"

The girl did her best to ignore him and strung her words

together even quicker than before. "The other man that was being dragged is an Injun. Miss Lin said that the Injun was the same one that everyone's been looking for."

Harden spun around and flew across the room so quickly that he startled the young girl. "What?" he snapped. "What Injun are you talking about? What else did Miss Lin say?"

Still very nervous, the girl appeared to be getting used to all the sudden movements within the suite. "She said that the Injun was the one who walked with the old man. She said he was the one that all those men were after and that he was coming back in town for the old man."

"And what about this stranger?" Harden asked. "The other one. What about him?"

To that, the girl only shrugged. "I don't know. He had a rope around the Injun's neck, just like I told you." She looked over to Elle and started backing toward the door. "Can I go now?"

It was Harden who answered her, and he used a voice almost as smooth as his silk suit. "Yes, you can," he said. "And take this with you." He dug in his pocket and pulled out a folded bundle of cash. Peeling off one of the bills, he handed it to the girl and winked. "That's for running up here so fast. I'll give you another if you keep watch on those two and tell me what else you see."

Suddenly, the girl didn't seem half as frightened anymore. She took the money Harden gave her and smiled widely. She nodded fiercely and spun around to look at Elle. The brunette let her know it was okay by nodding as well.

"I will, mister," the girl said. "I certainly will."

And then the girl dashed out of the room. She was in such a hurry to earn another handout that she forgot to close the door behind her. Max stepped up and shut the door, making sure to lock it before turning around to face Harden.

"You want me to check this out?" he asked.

Harden nodded. "Yeah. And put word out that I want to talk to Abe. Sometimes he surfaces quicker when he gets the call from on high."

"Do you think this is really the Indian we're looking for?"

"Sounds like it, doesn't it? There's no harm in checking it out."

"And what about this other man bringing him in?"

"The one with the rope? By the sound of it, I'd say he's collecting on the reward I offered. He must be something if he got ahold of that damn Indian." Patting the holster under his arm, Harden added, "Let's just make sure he doesn't live long enough to collect."

TWENTY-TWO

Clint left the little hotel through the back door. At first, he wasn't even able to find the other exit in the shadowy hallway, until he was led there by one of the Chinese who'd been lurking in the darkness. Although not really protected by any kind of elaborate device, the door simply wasn't marked and didn't have a handle. Because of that, it couldn't really be seen until it was pushed open by an experienced hand.

The Chinese man who led Clint out all but shoved him through the door and then quickly closed it again. Clint was surprised at the strength in the smaller man's arm, since the top of his head only came up to a spot just above Clint's chin.

After the time he'd spent with Motega, however, Clint wasn't quick to judge another man strictly on their appearance. He thought he'd gotten over that particular shortcoming some time ago, but the Indian challenged his preconceptions even more. That also taught Clint a more valuable lesson.

Once he was outside, Clint looked at the back wall of the hotel and witnessed the door vanish almost completely in front of his eyes. The outline of the door blended in extremely well with the wall, which was kept grimy and soiled with soot to obscure the entrance.

As he looked, Clint heard a knocking on the other side of the door. There was one knock, a pause, and then two more quick knocks. Not only did the knocking rattle the door enough for Clint to see it better, but he also figured he should remember that sequence when he returned.

Clint walked around the building and cut across the back of the next building over, just to put some distance between himself and the hotel. When he emerged from the alley and stepped out onto the street, he looked quickly over to the hotel and spotted a few familiar faces walking or standing nearby.

As promised, not one of those faces looked back at him with anything remotely resembling recognition. In fact, Clint thought for a moment that he hadn't seen those faces before. His memory wasn't failing him, he knew. Instead, those Chinese guards were just very good at their job.

Clint didn't want to waste another moment. He went over to retrieve Eclipse from where he'd tied him off, and led the stallion by the reins toward the Oriental Palace. Now that he wasn't leading Motega at the end of a rope, he wasn't attracting a fraction of the attention as when he'd arrived. That was fine by Clint, since that part of the plan was over.

The message had been delivered.

Now he merely had to wait for someone to reply.

By the looks of things, Clint figured he wasn't going to have to wait very long at all.

"One nice thing about small towns," Clint said softly to himself as well as Eclipse. "Word travels fast."

The Darley Arabian shook his head and let out a huffing breath. Much like the man who rode him, the horse was sensitive to tensions that surrounded him. Most animals were like that. That was how they survived. After years of living in a harsh world, Clint had become like that, too. He could feel hostility in the air like the crackle of heat lightning and he sure as hell felt it just then.

"It's all right, boy. I know we're headed straight for trouble. Just rest up and be ready for me when I need you."

Clint spoke partially because the sound of his voice soothed Eclipse, but also to get things straight in his own mind. He was now in front of the Oriental Palace and close enough to pick out a nearby hitching post to tie up Eclipse. Having snapped the reins around the post and cinched them with a quick tug, Clint patted the stallion on the nose and headed for the front door.

The building was large and block-shaped, looming over him as though it looked down on Clint with its many windows for eyes. The Oriental Palace had rows of windows lining both its levels, some of which were stained-glass depictions of Chinese dragons or lilies. All of the windows except for one were covered with expensive looking curtains. The one that was uncovered was the largest window, directly next to the front door. That one had the name of the place painted in black letters in both English and Chinese.

The front entrance was closed off by twin, ornately carved doors sporting polished brass handles. Clint pulled open one of those doors and felt a wave of warm, scented air wash out over him. He could smell perfume mixed with tobacco smoke. A piano player filled the air with a slow, lilting melody that seemed almost as exotic as the Palace's interior.

Clint couldn't even begin to look at each different decorative piece in turn. There was so much crushed red velvet and so many gold-gilded edges that it all seemed to blend together into a single luxurious surface. There were women everywhere he looked, reclining on sofas, sitting in chairs or even just walking about from one side of the room to another. As soon as they spotted Clint in the doorway, several of the ladies made their way over to him.

Although most of them were Chinese, a few of the girls had a more Western appearance. Each of them, however, was exotic in her own particular way. One of them especially struck Clint's eye since her skin was darker than any of the rest. She was one of the few who didn't move to greet him. Instead, she remained stretched out on a plush sofa, her muscled legs tucked up underneath the rest of her exquisite body.

Instinctually, Clint changed his direction and began heading straight for the girl with the smooth, chocolate brown skin. Her hair was short and tied behind her head, and she was dressed in a white camisole that made her seem all the more luscious and appealing.

"Please come in," came a voice from outside of Clint's field of vision. The one who'd spoken was another woman, who was walking down a set of wide stairs that curved slightly toward the front doors. The voice was soft and sensual, yet powerful enough to be heard clearly where Clint was standing.

Standing midway down the stairs, wearing a thin silk robe wrapped around a scantily clad body, was a tall woman with flowing black hair. She moved down the stairs as though she was floating, her legs emerging from the robe clad in expensive silk stockings.

Once she was at the bottom of the staircase, she opened her arms and said, "Welcome to the Oriental Palace."

"You know," Clint said, looking around at all the women surrounding him. "I can't recall the last time I've ever felt more welcome."

TWENTY-THREE

The brunette stepped forward and offered Clint her hand. "My name is Elle. Just let me know if you see anything here that you like."

Clint took his time allowing his eyes to roam over Elle's body. She was almost as tall as him, but much of that height was due to a pair of black, high-heeled shoes she wore. Her legs seemed to flow up like a fine sculpture, enticing Clint through the open slit of her robe. He could just make out the top of one thigh and the ribbon that connected her stocking to a matching black garter.

Her torso was slender and lightly muscled. Fine, firm breasts filled out a thin, lacy top. That was all Clint could make out before she pulled her robe tighter around herself. She tossed a strand of hair over her shoulder and regarded him with wide, dark green eyes.

"I can tell you've already found something to your liking," Elle said.

Clint nodded. "You've got that right."

"Then why don't you stay awhile? Can I take your hat and coat?"

Clint had had just enough time to remove his hat when he felt several small hands moving over his upper body.

Surprised at first, he saw that the girls around him were sliding their hands over his back, shoulders and ribs, massaging him gently while slipping their fingers beneath his coat. They peeled the coat off him with expert precision and handed it to one of the girls who seemed too young to do more than run errands.

"Actually, I came by to talk to someone," Clint said.

A slender Chinese woman with lips painted like rubies slid herself against him while running her hands over his chest. "We can talk all you want. Then we do much more. Whatever you like."

Clint started to push the Chinese woman away, but couldn't get himself to follow through once he got his hands on her shoulder. She felt so soft and so inviting that he let his hand wander down until he could pat her once on the bottom.

"Maybe later," he finally said. "Actually, I was hoping to find someone named Albert Harden."

When they heard that name, most of the women moved back to distance themselves from Clint. A few stepped back farther than the rest, but they all suddenly lost the professional flirtatiousness they'd used to greet him.

Elle was the only one who seemed unaffected by hearing that name. In fact, she moved through a gap created by the wall of women until she was close enough to whisper and still be heard by Clint.

"And who may I say is here?" she asked.

"Clint Adams. I've got something that he's been after for a while."

"Does he know you?"

"Maybe. I know a lot of people."

As she spoke to him, Elle kept her eyes locked onto Clint's and reached out to rub both hands along his ribs and down to his hips. "Do you want to see him now or would you like to take a moment for yourself?"

"It seems like I've spooked most of your employees here."

Elle's body pushed up against him. She moved one leg out so she could brush it against Clint's outer thigh, opening her robe just enough for him to get a nice, lingering view of her scantily clad body. "I wasn't talking about them," she said, moving her breasts over Clint's chest. "I could take care of you just fine."

The sensation of Elle's firm body pressed against his moved through Clint like a flush of heat beneath his skin. His body reacted to her closeness as well as the scent of her lightly perfumed hair. Elle immediately felt what she was doing to him and gently brushed the warm spot between her legs against his crotch.

"That's a tempting offer," he said without the slightest bit of exaggeration. "But you know how the saying goes. Business before pleasure."

Reluctantly, Elle pulled herself away from him. She let her hands stay on him for as long as possible until even her fingertips had to be taken away from his body. It seemed as though she was another piece of clothing that was being slowly stripped off of him.

"Suit yourself," she whispered. "But I can't guarantee this offer will be around for much longer."

This time, Clint reached forward and put his hands on her hips. He curled his fingers in just enough to keep her from moving away another inch and ran his hands down along the supple curve of her waist. "Maybe not," he told her. "But I should be able to keep it open for a while."

Elle did her best to keep her expression from changing as Clint's hands slowly peeled away from her body. The only thing she couldn't control, however, was the hunger that welled up in her eyes and the energy that caused her muscles to tense ever so slightly beneath her skin.

When Clint finally did take his hands away, he saw the brunette let out a slow, deep breath. Her cheeks flushed

slightly and the tip of her tongue darted out to moisten
her upper lip.

"I'll go up to let Mr. Harden know you're here," she
said, turning on the balls of her feet and walking toward
the stairs. "Wait here and I'll come to get you if he feels
like talking."

Clint waited for her to start climbing the staircase before he said, "Tell him I've got the Indian that's been
giving his men the slip. That should make him feel like
talking."

As he figured, those words stopped Elle in her tracks.
She picked up her pace and started up the steps once
again. "I'll tell him. Don't move from that spot. I'm sure
he'll want to see you right away."

Clint watched her climb the stairs, admiring the way
Elle's tight backside moved back and forth with every
step. Her heels could be heard knocking against the carpeted wood until the piano player picked up his tune from
where he'd left off a few moments ago.

Elle disappeared upstairs for less than a minute before
showing up once again and leaning over the upper balcony. "Come on up, Mr. Adams. Mr. Harden would like
to have a word with you."

Heading for the staircase, Clint smiled and said, "I'll
just bet he would."

TWENTY-FOUR

Staying indoors and out of sight was the smartest thing to do. Motega knew that. But no matter how many times he thought it over, he couldn't fight back the yearning that tore at him like an animal trying to claw its way out from inside his stomach.

The room he'd been given had one door and no windows. Because of that, it was safe and easy to guard from inside or out. But that also made the room feel like a jail cell to the Indian, who had become all too accustomed to roaming freely with the great sky stretched out over his head.

Actually, the more he thought about the sky above him and the soil below, the more the room felt less like a jail cell and more like a coffin. Once he reached that point in his mind, the yearning became too strong to bear.

He had to get out.

There was no question about it. Staying locked up in that wooden box seemed worse than facing an army of gunmen. The last straw was when he remembered a lesson he'd learned from Master Po.

"A man will always find himself in danger," the old

Chinese man had told him. "Much of that danger is lifted once the man knows it is there."

Motega knew leaving the safety of the hotel was dangerous. Therefore, he would be sure to keep his wits about him once he stepped through the door. Feeling better the instant he stepped out into the dark hallway, Motega stretched his arms and legs before heading for the back entrance.

"You know better than that," Tam warned him from the counter at the opposite end of the hall.

Motega nodded once and said, "Yes, I do. But if there is danger lurking right outside this door, then surely it would have come through it sooner or later."

Tam shook his head and waved a frustrated hand toward the Indian. "That old fool Po has filled your head with double-talk and nonsense. Just try not to walk too far. I'll do my best to warn you before someone comes to claim your head."

"Thank you, Tam."

The old Chinese man acknowledged Motega's thanks with a grumbling sigh. He wasn't happy about the Indian leaving the hotel, but he also knew it would be useless to try and stop him. So rather than waste the effort, Tam motioned to one of the nearby guards and said, "Keep an eye on him."

The guard nodded once, waited for Motega to leave through the back door and then followed in his tracks.

It felt good to step outside and feel the cold air once again brush over his face. Although it had been less than an hour since he'd last been in the open winds, Motega felt as though he'd been cooped up for days. He didn't always have such an aversion to being inside, but the circumstances of recent times had put an extra sense of urgency into his soul.

Motega was an animal pursued and felt very much the

part. Merely stepping outside when he knew it was all but forbidden was enough to make the Indian feel in control of his own destiny once again. Such a thing did him a world of good, no matter what other dangers came along with it.

Words from his master were drifting through his mind, as they often did, but they suddenly stopped as Motega froze where he stood. Every one of his muscles tensed, and the wintry cold was pushed aside as his blood pumped through his veins at a quicker rate.

There was someone else nearby and it wasn't one of Tam's men. The men who guarded the hotel and those under Tam's protection moved with a certain silent fluidity. What Motega heard was someone moving quickly, who wasn't as proficient in hiding their presence as someone who'd trained for years in that subtle art.

Although he didn't move, the Indian instinctively checked for his weapons by feeling where they brushed against his body. The cold touch of steel was right where it should be, as was the familiar presence of a solid wooden handle.

A breath remained at the top of his lungs, waiting until it was safe for the Indian to release it. Even as his heart thumped within his chest, Motega didn't budge a fraction of an inch. Not even a trace of steam drifted from his mouth or nostrils.

Suddenly, the quiet that had settled around him was shattered by an explosion of sound and motion. It came from the alley closest to where Motega was standing, and the figure who charged toward him moved as though he'd been shot out of a cannon wedged between the two closest buildings.

For a moment, Motega couldn't get a look at what was coming at him. He knew it had to be a man simply because it walked on two legs and was covered in leather clothing. Apart from that, the figure moved, snarled and

even smelled like an animal. Its arms and legs sprung
forward as it let out a growling, angry voice.

"I got you now, you Injun son of a bitch!" the man-
beast hollered.

Now that he was no longer trying to make any attempt
at stealth, the hulking figure fueled its motion with pure
fury. The effect was similar to dumping kerosene onto an
already raging fire.

Motega had been charging himself up as well, only in
a way much different than his attacker. He'd felt the burst
of fear and instinctual panic that any other person would,
but he saved that up inside of him until he was ready to
burn it off.

He waited until the last possible moment to do that, but
when he did, his body was ready to follow up on whatever
Motega demanded of it. Judging by the crazed look in the
other man's eyes, Motega was going to need all the inner
fire he could find.

TWENTY-FIVE

Crouching down slightly, the Indian bent his knees and then shot himself forward like a trap that had been sprung. He launched himself up into a tight midair somersault and landed with both feet on the ground, the rest of his body crouching down low into a compact bundle. As soon as he felt his chest press against his knees, he sensed a rush of air over his head.

The Indian's reflexive need to drop down low whenever he was attacked kept him this time from getting his head knocked off his shoulders by a massive, swinging fist. A sound like a log being hurtled through the air followed the gust of wind, and the raging man nearly stumbled with the effort of the mighty swing.

Abe's face was as red as his hair. His lips were parted into a snarl that was drenched in saliva. "Stand up, you fucking frog, and fight like a man."

Once again, Motega gathered all the energies that were flowing through him. He used all his emotion and all of his excitement to push himself straight up into the air, as though he'd been standing on top of a coiled spring.

His head came up first and shot past Abe's chin in a blur of motion. His body followed quickly after as Motega

lifted his arms up over his head. The Indian's back began
to curve away from Abe as his knees and legs rose up off
the ground. As soon as his knees were up past stomach
level, Motega arched back even further, until he formed
a crescent shape in midair.

All of this happened so quickly that Abe barely had a
chance to react. By the time he started reaching out to
snatch the Indian into a devastating bear hug, Abe heard
the familiar sound of something solid slicing through the
air.

It was Motega's legs that were cutting through the air,
and they were both snapping up and around like two ends
of a whip that was just about to snap. When the Indian's
hands landed palms down against the earth, he pulled his
legs inward and waited until the last moment before
straightening his knees.

The maneuver ended with Motega's feet whipping up
and around, and slamming into Abe's jaw with enough
force to take all the wind from the redhead's sails. Using
his stomach muscles to pull himself over, Motega pushed
off with his hands so he could once again land on his feet.
As soon as he hit the ground, he brought his head up to
look at what his opponent was doing.

Howling in pain, Abe staggered a few steps back while
lifting his hands to cover his face. He could feel a fiery
agony that filled up his entire skull as he let out his snarl-
ing cry. The pain came from trying to move his jaw,
which had been broken by the impact of Motega's double
kick. Even as his mouth filled with blood, Abe managed
to keep himself from backing up more than a step and
quickly pulled himself together.

He realized his jaw was broken a split second before
pressing his hands against his face. Abe shook his head
and swallowed the pain that followed. Now that he knew
how much damage had been done, he shoved the pain to

the back of his mind and used it to focus even harder on
his target.

At that moment, the back door to the hotel flew open
and the guard sent by Tam to watch over Motega shot
outside. The slim Chinese man saw what was going on
and immediately pulled a knife that had been hanging at
his side. He could tell Abe was wounded, so he charged
forward with the blade held out in front of him.

Motega was ready to launch another attack of his own,
but stopped halfway through it when the guard ran in front
of him. Not wanting to waste one precious second, the
Indian reached beneath the layer of thin leather covering
his torso and removed one of the weapons he kept there.
The knife had a short, curved blade and a handle that had
been specially carved to fit his hand. As soon as his fingers closed around the weapon, Motega was moving to
get around the guard.

Although Abe had been staggering backward with a
face covered in fresh blood, his eyes were still clear and
his breath was still surging strongly through his lungs. If
the guard had noticed that, he might have thought twice
about throwing himself toward the redheaded giant so
quickly.

But it was too late for second-guessing.

Abe's mouth twisted into a crooked, painful smile as
he realized that very thing.

With a speed that seemed almost impossible from
someone who'd taken a kick strong enough to break his
jaw, Abe reached out with his left hand to clamp a fist
around the approaching guard's throat. Thick, beefy fingers dug deeply into the Chinese man's neck while Abe's
other hand drew the .44 stuffed beneath his belt.

Pulling the smaller man in a little closer, Abe took in
a deep breath and spat a mouthful of blood into the
guard's face. "Vug you, jinaman," he slurred with his
skewed jaw.

From there, Abe brought up his pistol and jabbed it into the guard's belly. The smaller man's body jerked as a muffled shot thumped through the air and the .44-caliber bullet exploded out of the guard's back. A red mist plumed out from the smoking wound and the guard's body went limp, but Abe pulled his trigger once again just to be sure.

Another explosion and another spray of gore erupted from the body before Abe let it drop and turned his attention toward Motega.

The Indian was already there and nearly close enough to bury his knife into Abe's side. There wasn't much room to maneuver since Abe had been backed into the opening of the alley, but Motega used his speed to his advantage.

Building up to a run in the space of five paces, Motega leapt up off of one foot and pressed his other against a nearby wall. He immediately pushed off the wall and launched himself at Abe, the blade in his hand slicing toward the other man's exposed ribs.

The redhead twisted his upper body and swatted Motega down with a crushing backhand. He'd caught some of the blade in the meat of his arm, but was too enraged to feel it. Instead, he brought the .44 around and sighted quickly down its barrel.

"You're negst, Injun," Abe snarled, his jaw refusing to budge. "Time to die."

TWENTY-SIX

Motega was still on the ground when he saw the back door of the hotel swing open once again. This time, two of Tam's men were about to come out, but they weren't going to be as hasty as the one who'd gone before them.

Both of the men took a moment to look at what was going on. The first thing they spotted was Abe towering over the fallen Indian. Next, they caught sight of the bloodied corpse of the first guard who'd come rushing out to help. As soon as they saw that body, their faces darkened and they moved out to extract their revenge.

"No," Motega shouted from where he was laying. "Stay back."

Neither of the two took a single step back into the hotel. Out of respect for Motega, however, they didn't move forward either. Instead, they held their ground and waited for the first reason to throw themselves at the enraged attacker.

Abe watched this exchange with some amusement. The gun in his hand had drifted to a point halfway between Motega and the hotel's door. Now that he saw that the other guards weren't going to come at him after all, he grinned and spat some more blood to the ground.

"Jus' like a jinaman," Abe slurred. "Yellow inside an' oud."

Before Abe could finish his insult, Motega leaned back onto his hands, pushed up with his legs and brought his whole body upright with a powerful kick. His torso coiled forward like a serpent's and the blade wavered back and forth like a scorpion's stinger.

"Thas more lige id. The Injun's god some fight in 'im."

Motega snapped his hand forward and to the right, only to pull it quickly back and make his true strike on the left. Abe fell for the initial baiting maneuver and went to block it, leaving himself open for the Indian's second swipe.

Seeing that his blade was going to find its target, Motega thought quickly enough to take advantage of it. His hand slashed out and across, tearing into Abe's ribs and continuing outward while his body twisted into a tight spiral. The tip of the blade left a stream of blood hanging in the air as Motega turned all the way around until he'd completed a full circle.

The Indian's knife arm had wrapped partially around his torso, until it was as tight as it could get. From there, he snapped it out and slashed with the knife again, aiming for roughly the same spot he'd hit the first time. Even though the second strike came less than a second after the first, Motega's knife didn't make it to Abe's torso.

The hulking redhead brought up his arm and swung it forward, catching Motega's arm just beneath the elbow. He put all of his muscle into the block and smashed away the incoming strike, while letting out a feral growl. In fact, Abe seemed even more amused by the show Motega was giving him and had yet to feel the pain of his fresh wound.

"Yeah!" Abe snarled. He was so wrapped up in the moment that he opened his mouth when he spoke. The pain that caused sent another wave of fire through his skull and neck, but Abe merely used that to drive himself onward.

Blood seeped from his side as Abe balled up his fist and used his blocking arm to lash out with another backhand. His knuckles caught Motega on the cheek, but glanced off rather than sank in with their full power.

Motega rolled with the punch, allowing his head to snap to the side. He even let his upper body sway backward to take away some of the strike's momentum, but Abe's knuckles still left Motega slightly dizzy. Mainly, he was surprised that the other man could take so much punishment. Never before had Motega hit with such solid blows without putting his opponent out of the fight.

Not only was he still in the fight, but Abe was actually enjoying himself. The sight, smell and taste of his own blood had thrown him into a kind of frenzy that was truly frightening to watch. His eyes were wild and yet focused. His body moved with savage efficiency as he followed up his backhand by bringing his .44 straight forward to point at Motega's chest.

The gun moved as though it was a part of Abe's fist. Its steel finger pointed at its target before spitting out a plume of fiery smoke. It bucked against Abe's palm, filling the alley with another explosive blast.

Motega was still rolling with the backhand, using every one of his senses to try and guess what Abe might do next. He'd managed to catch a glimpse of the gun barrel as it came toward him and reacted the only way he could at the moment. The Indian stepped back with one foot and continued twisting his body while stepping to one side.

When the gun went off, Motega could feel the heat from the blast like the tongue of a dragon from one of Master Po's stories. Using his own momentum instead of his muscles, he snapped his body around until he felt the hot lead rip through his skin.

That bullet tore through the Indian's leather tunic and scraped along his flesh. Since he'd managed to take that step back and turn in less time than it took to blink, Motega suffered no more than a scratch as the bullet hissed onward and sparked against the wall behind him.

When he planted his foot again, Motega looked down at his left side to see the blackened tear in his leathers, which was tainted with a trickle of blood. He snapped his eyes up to look at Abe just as the redhead was lining up another shot.

Motega knew he had less than a heartbeat to decide what to do next. He used that time to let out a quick breath and snap his hand back and then quickly forward. The blade flew from his grip like a spark, whirling through the air with a hissing sound similar to a bullet.

Rather than try to dodge the blade that was heading straight for his gun hand, Abe moved his arm up just enough to put the .44 out of the knife's path. His maniacal grin took on an even wilder quality when Abe felt the blade thump into his forearm just the way he'd wanted.

"Now whad you gonna do?" Abe sneered. Motega's knife was lodged solidly in his flesh, wavering slightly from the impact. "And I heard you was so fugging tough."

For the first time in years, Motega stared at an opponent in wide-eyed wonder. He'd hit the redhead with enough to drop three men, but this one was still coming. Something unfamiliar slipped into the Indian's gut just then: fear.

TWENTY-SEVEN

Elle waited for Clint to get up the stairs before she walked away from the balcony to meet him. She brushed her robe over her so that it covered most of her body as she moved. She left it open just enough for her long legs to appear through the slit when she walked, and judging by the way she walked, she knew exactly what she was showing him.

Clint admired the display, knowing that it was being put on solely for his benefit. He knew when a woman was using her own body to divert his attention or steer him a certain way. That didn't mean he couldn't enjoy the show while he followed her down the hall.

"This way," Elle said, pointing toward a nearby door.

Just as she said that, the door she'd motioned to opened and a man with light brown hair stepped into the hall. He was of average height and build, displaying the gun on his hip as though he thought he could impress Clint as well.

"Mr. Harden isn't in there, Elle," Max said. "Not anymore."

Clint noticed that the brunette looked genuinely surprised by the other man's statement. She stopped short and glanced at the man in the doorway and then back at Clint.

Quickly regaining her composure, she said, "But he was just—"

Max nodded crisply and smiled. "Yeah, he was. He's not anymore. Aren't you going to introduce us?"

"Max Emery," Elle said, stepping back so her shoulder nearly bumped against the wall. "This is Clint Adams."

Max stepped forward and extended his hand. "Clint Adams? I think I've heard of you."

"Really? Well, I'm almost flattered."

"Mr. Harden would like to talk to you in his office, where he conducts his more important business. Right this way."

After Max had walked past him and headed for a room at the opposite end of the hall, Clint glanced over to Elle one last time. Years of playing poker had made him an expert in reading faces, and it was no chore at all to pick out the fact that the brunette was puzzled by what Max was doing. His guess was that she was either one hell of an actress or Elle hadn't known Max was going to show up at all.

Clint got that much from her in an instant. Rather than make it obvious that he thought he might know something other than what he'd been told, he tipped his hat to her and said, "Hopefully we'll meet up again. Maybe after Mr. Harden is done with me?"

If Clint hadn't known exactly what to look for, he would have missed the odd expression on Elle's face. She quickly wiped most of it away and returned Clint's smile.

"Definitely," she said with a flirtatiousness that seemed slightly forced compared to how it had been before Max showed up. "I'm not through with you yet."

"Glad to hear it." With that, Clint turned on his heels and followed in Max's footsteps.

The man in the brown suit was waiting at a door at the

end of the hall. He seemed to be losing his patience, but pushed his lips into a polite smile when he saw that Clint was about to catch up. He then opened the door and motioned for Clint to walk through it.

Clint stopped and looked through the door, to find that it opened onto the top of a narrow flight of stairs.

"This leads to a room reserved for the Palace's most distinguished clients," Max explained. "Perhaps if things go well, Mr. Harden may treat you to a night there with one of our ladies."

"We'll see."

"Go on, then. Straight down to the bottom and through the door."

"Aren't you coming?" Clint asked when he saw Max step back from the door.

"I'm not invited. All I do is point the way."

Max was doing a good job of being courteous. He smiled like he meant it and spoke without a tremble in his voice. In fact, if Clint hadn't been able to get such a good look at Elle's face, he might have bought into the idea that Mr. Harden was indeed happy to see him and that business was going right on schedule.

Then again, Clint had been led around by too many smug little pricks like this Max Emery to buy into anything they said. He could recognize them from a mile away, and all Elle had done was put his mind at ease that his initial judgment of the man was correct.

But there was no reason for Max to know that any of that was going through Clint's mind. On the contrary, Clint thought about all of this as he walked down the stairs, acting completely oblivious to anything that might be going on behind the scenes.

That had been a part of his plan. Just so long as they were confident enough in themselves to let Clint keep his gun, the plan was going even better than Clint might have hoped. It wasn't until Clint had walked by him that Max seemed to brighten up for a moment, as though something had just dawned on him.

Perhaps he had finally remembered why Clint's name sounded familiar.

Perhaps he just realized that he'd forgotten to disarm Clint before allowing him to walk through that door.

Or maybe he was just able to recognize a shark in the water, just as Clint could recognize the bait.

Whichever it was, Clint would have to think about it later. For the moment, he had much other important matters on his mind. The first of which was exactly when the trap was going to be sprung.

He could smell the trap, but Clint figured that he'd been through enough of them to make it through this one as well. Just as long as Motega was safe, he doubted this Harden person would do too much on their first meeting. Maybe try to put a fright into him or threaten him for a bit before turning him loose.

There was only one way to truly find out how this was going to play out. Focusing on the reassuring weight of the Colt which hung at his side, Clint climbed down the rest of the stairs as the upper door was shut and locked.

TWENTY-EIGHT

The stairs went down to the first floor, leading to a door similar to the one at the top of the flight. Clint opened that door and took a moment to soak in his surroundings. The room was fairly open and seemed every bit as plush yet tawdry as one might expect from a private suite stashed away inside a whorehouse.

Every inch of floor was covered with thick red carpet, and tapestries hung on every wall. Stepping into the room, Clint noticed that the large bed and small bar didn't even take up half of the space. There wasn't a single bare board to be seen, making the sound of Clint's footsteps fade quickly, as it was absorbed into the lavish material surrounding him.

Expensive candle holders were spaced evenly throughout the room, giving the place a warm, sumptuous feel. The smell of perfume and flowers was in the air, but neither scent was fresh. There were no flowers to be seen, and no fragrances had been sprayed into the air. The room merely kept those scents within it, much the way a funeral parlor retained the smell of death.

Once inside the room, Clint stopped and looked around one last time to make sure there wasn't anyone waiting

112

to step in behind him or from either side. All he saw was more covered walls and another set of flickering candles.

The only other person in there with him was a man who stood at the other end of the room with his back to Clint and his hands clasped behind him. That solitary figure stood motionless for another couple of seconds, until Clint had had a chance to take in all the eye-catching decorations of the private suite.

Clint felt an uneasiness settle into his stomach and couldn't quite put his finger on where it had come from. Then he realized that he could hear nothing else inside the room. He couldn't even hear any sounds from the other side of the wall.

In any structure, the walls couldn't hold back voices or the thumping of feet against the floor or the occasional slamming of a door. In this room, however, there was no sound at all. Suddenly, Clint felt as though the room existed somewhere miles away from any town or any other living thing.

"Hello there," Clint said, wanting to get this part of the plan over with as soon as possible. "My name is—"

"I know who you are," the man at the other end of the room said. Just like Clint's footsteps, the man's voice sounded and then was immediately soaked up by the carpets and tapestries. "I must say, I didn't think you would come down here so quickly."

"Sorry to disappoint you, Mr. Harden. I just wanted to meet with you first, since I figured you'd be most interested in what I have to offer."

"What you have to offer?" the other man repeated with mild amusement. "And what would that be?"

"An Indian that got away from you not too long ago. From what I hear, he was traveling with an old Chinese man. I don't know all the details, but I do know he was tough to get a rope around. Once I did, he seemed to calm down well enough."

The other man nodded slowly. He was dressed in black silk pants and wore a black vest over a clean white shirt. The hands clasped behind him were thin and well maintained. His hair was so black that it almost shimmered in the light. He was looking at an intricate tapestry on the wall directly in front of him. The scene depicted a ghostly figure woven in silvery thread talking to a woman standing in an empty field.

"And since when did the great Clint Adams stoop to collecting rewards for fugitive slaves?" the man asked without turning around to look at Clint.

Clint took another step forward and slowly moved around the room. He kept his steps cautious and slow while trying to get a better look at the other man's face. "I don't go looking for jobs like this. It just happened to come my way. A man's got to earn his money somehow."

"And I suppose you earn your money by riding into a situation that has nothing to do with you and choosing sides without knowing every detail? You earn money by sitting back and watching while four other men are beaten into submission so you can ride off with the victor? Is that how you earn your money, Mr. Clint Adams?"

Clint stopped right where he was. Every instinct inside of him told him that something was very wrong in that room. "What else do you know about how I earn my living?"

"I know that you and the New Arrow are working together to free Master Po. And I also know that you walked into this town thinking no man in here could keep you from walking out."

"That's how a man in my line of work stays alive, Mr. Harden."

"You are wrong on two counts, Mr. Adams," the man said as he spun around so quickly that his silk clothing snapped. "I am not Mr. Harden and you will most definitely not leave this place alive."

TWENTY-NINE

Motega's body was filled with a sudden burst of energy that was equal parts adrenaline and desperation. Using methods to control the flow of his own energies, the Indian pumped blood through his body the way steam was pumped through a train's engine.

He could control his heartbeat and slow it down just enough to keep himself from tiring out too quickly.

He could control his breathing so that every other part of him could move more quickly and efficiently.

The one thing he could not seem to control was the man who would not stop attacking him, no matter how much damage he took or how much blood he lost. That was where, no matter how hard Motega tried to fight them back, the fear and desperation came into play.

It hadn't taken long for the two guards waiting in the hotel doorway to break Motega's command and come running into the battle. The first one made it close enough to get one hand on Abe's shoulder before the redhead twisted around and slammed an elbow into the guard's face. The blow landed squarely on the other man's nose, smashing cartilage and bone into pulp, dropping the guard half a second later.

115

Motega flew forward with a flurry of short kicks and powerful, jabbing punches. One after another, his strikes landed, but none of them seemed to have any effect whatsoever on his opponent. Although he knew he was doing damage, Motega didn't feel Abe pulling back or easing up one bit. Instead, the redhead's eyes focused more on him, and his return attacks became more vicious.

The third guard took a backhand in the face, but recovered fairly quickly. When he stabbed his knife toward Abe, the redhead deflected the blow using the side of his gun. From there, it was just a matter of turning his wrist and pulling his trigger to blow a hole through the other man's heart.

Feeling the spray of warm blood on his face made Abe's smile grow even wider. Like a devil amid the damned, Abe was in his element. He would feel pain and bruises later. Now there was only time enough to revel in the death he'd caused.

Motega had seen the gun coming around to point at the guard, but was unable to do anything before that trigger was pulled. Now that it was too late to save that particular life, Motega pushed himself to another level of intensity in his own attacks.

He landed two punches and a solid thrust kick before Abe could even take his eyes away from the two guards he'd dropped. The muscle Motega felt was like cast iron beneath the redhead's skin. Abe had himself so tensed that it was a wonder he could even move.

Any doubt as to that question was quickly thrown out when Abe turned around and swung his pistol toward Motega. His arm sliced through the air like a piece of lumber, and at the end of it the pistol was ready to be fired.

Motega had himself calmed a bit and had the presence of mind to see the attack before it got there. Lifting both hands, he blocked the incoming arm and pushed it away as Abe's pistol spat another round into the air.

The bullet hissed into empty space, but Abe was already preparing to fire again. Motega could tell as much just by reading the other man's eyes and feeling how his body was moving. In the second he had left, the Indian raised one arm and brought it down in a swift, straight line. At the same time, he lifted one of his legs to smash Abe's wrist in between his knee and elbow.

Motega's combined blows landed on target, impacting with such force that he could feel them land through the wrist that was wedged in between his arm and leg. The Indian let out a sharp, piercing yell that allowed him to drain some of the tension inside of him, as well as the fear that had been building up.

Sucking in a ragged breath, Abe tried to pull his arm free, but could not get out from between Motega's elbow and knee. When he exhaled, he let out a loud snarl of his own, spraying as a final insult the blood that had collected in his mouth. With what little slack he'd gotten, Abe reared back and then twisted forward.

It didn't take an expert in the fighting arts to see the redhead's second arm speeding toward Motega. Watching every move Abe made, Motega saw the blow coming from a mile away. Unfortunately, since he wasn't too anxious to let Abe's gun hand free, there wasn't much of anywhere for Motega to go.

All the Indian could do was lean back, while bringing his free arm up to guard his face and side. He also tensed his body in preparation for what he knew was coming next. Sure enough, Abe's fist pounded into his midsection like a rock that had been dropped from a cliff.

Even though he'd prepared to absorb the blow, Motega was still nearly leveled by the sheer brute force behind Abe's fist. All the wind flew from Motega's lungs and he was forced to drop his other leg just to keep from falling over.

Now that his hand was free, Abe pulled it away and

shook it back and forth to get the blood flowing through it once again. He was already tightening his grip around his pistol, picking out where on Motega's body he wanted to put the bullet..

Motega took a brief moment to collect himself as well. Merely trying to breathe hurt almost as much as that last punch. Every move he made brought on a specific pain of its own, but the Indian still wasn't about to give up.

Unfortunately, Abe didn't look as if he was going to quit anytime soon either. The Indian didn't know how Abe was doing it, but he was somehow keeping all the pain and fatigue in the back of his brain. Even Master Po hadn't been able to fight through such adversity with so few ill effects.

Rather than try to figure out that puzzle just then, Motega found one last thing he could do against his crazed, seemingly unbeatable adversary. He picked out a spot on Abe's side where the clothing was sliced open and the skin had been cut.

It was the spot that Motega had opened with his knife. He knew that if he didn't turn the redhead away with this one last attack, then things were going to take a drastic turn for the worse. Motega had considerable ability, but he also knew his limits.

This fight had to end quickly, he thought, while straightening his first and index fingers and forming them into one solid line. He had to think of this man as a wall which only had one breach in sight. Motega tensed those two fingers, drew his arm back, and then snapped it straight out again while taking a quick step forward.

Abe could almost feel the gun bucking in his hand and could almost smell the smoke curling up from the barrel. Suddenly, he felt something altogether different. It was a sharp impact in his ribs, followed by a pain so intense that it caused his vision to blur and his legs to buckle. His fingers tightened out of reflex, sending his last bullet into the wall behind Motega.

When he looked down, Abe could see the Indian with his fist still pressed against his side as though he'd been frozen there after delivering his punch. The pain hadn't stopped, however. In fact, it blasted through every one of Abe's senses, exploding once again, in a way that took out all the fury from his soul.

Then Motega pulled his hand away. Not only had he landed a punch on Abe's knife wound, but he'd driven two of his fingers into the wound, where they did even more damage inside before being pulled out again. Blood dripped from the Indian's fingers and he stepped back to prepare for Abe's next move.

When he felt those rock-hard fingers ripped out of his wound, Abe also felt the pain that he'd been holding back through the entire fight. His gun was empty and he felt like a piece of bloody, tenderized beef. He didn't fall over, though. Instead, he put Motega and the hotel behind him and walked away.

THIRTY

Clint had been on the lookout for danger from the moment he'd stepped out of Tam's hotel. No matter how hard he looked, there was no way he could have seen what was coming for him before the man in front of him exploded into a blur of motion.

It was sheer instinct that allowed Clint to throw himself to one side just as the other man threw a kick that sliced through the air where he'd just been standing. Clint's dodge wasn't graceful, but it got him out of the way in time. That was fortunate indeed, since the other man's foot slammed into the door leading to the stairs and shattered the solid wood.

Landing on his free foot, the other man craned his head around to look at Clint, while slowly pulling his other leg from the broken door.

Now that his mind had snapped into a quicker pace, Clint adjusted his balance and lunged forward to take back the offensive before the other man got a chance to attack again.

Clint thundered toward the door like a runaway train and lashed out with his hand in a simple yet powerful right hook. The punch had every bit of Clint's muscle behind it and sped nearly as fast as the other man's kick. But even though he hardly seemed to move, the other man ducked down low and avoided the punch entirely.

Now was the first time that Clint got a good opportunity to get a look at the other man's face. His skin had the shading of Chinese descent, but was somewhat darker around the eyes. His hair was so black that it seemed oily, yet it flowed like feathers around his face when he moved. His body was lithe and agile like a cat's, and he moved as though he believed the laws of gravity didn't apply to him.

"That was impressive," he said. "Especially for one so dependent on machines to do your fighting."

"I don't even know who you are," Clint said. "And there's no way you can know everything about me."

"I am called Raven. It will be remembered as the name of the man who defeated the great Gunsmith."

"You're not the first person to make that claim," Clint said, lashing out with a follow-up punch.

Raven twisted at the waist and shoulders until he was contorted in just a way for Clint's fist to sail past him without even brushing his clothes. While he was there, he snapped his left hand straight out, driving the tip of one finger deep into Clint's midsection.

The strike caught him in the middle of his solar plexus, immediately forcing all the air from Clint's lungs and sending ripples of pain throughout his entire body. As his vision started to blur, Clint saw a smile form on Raven's face. In all the fights Clint had been in, he couldn't recall feeling so much pain from one single blow.

Raven took his time freeing himself from the door, and even walked around the spot where Clint was standing. His eyes moved over Clint like a painter looking for the exact spot to place his brush. When he decided, he snapped his hand out again, this time jabbing a point along Clint's upper ribs and just under his arm.

Just as he'd been about to recover from the first jab, Clint felt the second one drive into him like a knife. The nerves on that entire side erupted with pain, sending jagged, invisible claws all the way through his chest. Clint's eyes widened as the pain reached a new level. His body was starting to go numb, and in a matter of time he knew he wouldn't be able to do much of anything to defend himself.

Raven seemed to be enjoying himself and kept circling Clint while looking for his next target. "You made a mistake in choosing this fight. I was hoping you would leave Motega to his own fate, but now you must share the same end as he."

"What fate is that?" Clint asked, trying to buy a moment or two to pull himself together.

"It is his fate to die at my hand, bringing his tale full circle. I'm sorry that his circle must close around you as well."

Clint had sucked in enough of a breath to get the feeling back into his right arm and torso. That wasn't much, but it was all he could get before Raven did even more damage. Clint tensed his muscles in his gun arm and prepared to make his move.

"If there's something you want me to tell Motega," Clint said. "I'll be happy to relay the message."

"That's quite all right, Mr. Adams. I'll tell him right before I take his life." With that, Raven planted his feet and drew back his hand like an arrow being drawn against the bow.

Having waited until the moment right before Raven's elbow had gone all the way back, Clint let out the breath he'd been holding and snapped his arm down toward the holster at his side. The motion wasn't the smoothest draw he'd ever made, but it was nearly as fast as Raven's first strike. In the space of a second, Clint's modified Colt had cleared leather and was coming up to aim at the man standing beside him.

Raven saw the draw just in time to reach down for the gun before its barrel could point directly at him.

That was exactly what Clint had been waiting for, and it was then that he spent the rest of the energy he'd been saving deep down inside of him. Raven's fingers had just grazed the Colt's cylinder when Clint twisted his hand so that the pistol was being held in a sideways grip. From there, he aimed and squeezed the trigger.

The Colt roared and spat its hot lead from Clint's fist. Although he could smell the acrid smoke, Clint didn't see the first hint of blood from Raven. In fact, he didn't even see the other man standing where he'd been no less than a second ago.

Where Raven had been facing Clint before, he was now twisted to the side. The front of his shirt had a fresh tear going across his belly where the Colt's bullet had traveled. He'd moved so fast that Clint had missed it simply by allowing himself to blink.

Raven shifted his spearlike fingers to point at Clint's eye. He smiled at that moment, anticipating the glory of taking The Gunsmith's life.

THIRTY-ONE

Clint shifted his weight from one foot onto another, dropping his center of gravity down in a way that reminded him of how Motega had ducked a few punches on the day they'd met. He gritted his teeth and leaned back a bit, hoping that he hadn't just zigged when he should have zagged.

It felt as though Raven's fingers were carved from solid rock. They struck outward as Raven let out a hissing breath, only to graze off Clint's cheek and slice the rest of the way through empty air.

Just as Clint was about to put some distance between himself and the other man, he saw Raven look away and turn his face toward the door. Rather than waste precious time in looking to see what had caught Raven's attention, Clint leaned forward until he was close enough to drive his head forward and slam it into the other man's temple.

The move managed to catch Raven by surprise only because Clint hadn't thought of it until it was halfway done. He'd simply found himself close enough to strike, and his reflexes had taken over from there. The impact jostled the brain inside Clint's skull and sent a dull ringing through his ears.

Luckily, it appeared to have an even greater effect on Raven, since he blinked several times in quick succession while lifting his hands to his face. Suddenly, the air filled with another explosive roar, followed by the hiss of lead whipping through the air.

A gunshot.

Clint couldn't see where it had come from, but he knew that sound well enough to recognize it when he heard it. He instinctively dropped to the ground and rolled away from the door, and away from Raven as well. When he came to a stop, Clint saw that Raven had taken out a small dagger that had been hidden somewhere on his person and was cocking it back to throw toward the door.

His body acting just as quickly as his brain could command it, Clint took aim and squeezed off another round. This time, his bullet struck its target, sparking off the metal of Raven's dagger and sending it flying from his grasp.

Raven didn't let a single moment pass him by. He threw himself forward, flying toward the door as though he had sprouted the wings of his namesake. He'd darted out of Clint's sight and was almost to the stairs by the time his chipped dagger hit the floor.

Clint was upright and racing toward the door with renewed vigor. For the moment, he didn't allow himself to feel the pain of Raven's stinging blows. He didn't even allow himself to feel the exertion of pushing his muscles to their limits. The only thing on Clint's mind was getting his hands on Raven before the other man disappeared entirely.

His footsteps barely made a sound within the insulated room. The carpets and tapestries had even absorbed most of the noise from the gunshots. The smoke still hung in the air like a cloud, catching in Clint's mouth as he stormed through it on his way to the room's only door.

When he got there and turned the corner, Clint saw a

figure waiting for him at the bottom of the stairs. He damn near took a shot at that figure, but stopped himself when he saw that it wasn't Raven looking back at him with wide eyes and a stunned expression.

Without breaking his stride, Clint ran up to the figure and clamped a hand around its wrist so he could push the gun in its hand away. He kept his fingers locked and pushed the figure back against the wall. Sighting down the Colt's barrel, Clint quickly noticed that there was nobody else on the stairs.

The door at the top of the steps was swinging shut, allowing Clint to catch a quick glimpse of Raven's heel as he darted out of sight.

Having seen the other man's speed, Clint ran up the stairs even though he hated to charge headfirst into hostile territory. It was either that, however, or let this particular Raven fly away.

As he moved up the stairs, Clint tore the gun from the hand of the person who'd been standing at the bottom of the stairs. From there, he bolted up the stairs until he could see what was going on in the hallway above.

There was nobody up there except for a few startled faces peeking out from behind almost-closed doors. Clint caught a glimpse of Raven's shirt as the other man ducked out of a window which looked down onto the back of the Palace.

Clint dashed over to the window and watched as Raven dropped onto the ground and darted away. As far as Clint could tell, the other man must have used a first-floor awning to break his fall, before bouncing off of that and landing on the ground below. It had all happened so quickly that Raven was in the wind before Clint could even think about following him.

As much as he hated to admit to it, Clint knew that Raven was either long gone or lying in wait in an alley or around a nearby corner. Whichever it was, Clint knew it would have been anything but smart to try and track down the other man. As if to reinforce his decision, all of the pain from the fight was once again asserting itself against his body, making it hard for him even to breathe without wincing.

Clint leaned back from the window and jogged to the door at the end of the hall. Once there, he opened it and looked down the stairs to find that the person there had almost climbed all the way up to meet him.

"What the hell are you doing here?" Clint asked.

Elle rubbed her wrist and stepped through the door. "I didn't know that was going to happen, Clint. You've got to believe me on that."

"Well, do you know who that man was?"

She shook her head. "All I know is that Mr. Harden was trying to use me to get you killed. I may have done some things I'm not proud of, but I couldn't live with myself if I was a part of something like that. I wanted to do what I could to help you before something terrible happened."

Clint looked around and saw that the curious faces had gone, but heavier footsteps were approaching. "My business with Harden isn't finished, but it's going to have to wait. If you really want to help, take me out of here through some way except the front door."

THIRTY-TWO

Elle showed Clint a smaller rear staircase which led down to the kitchen. Hurrying down those steps, Clint was on his guard the entire way. There weren't any more people gunning for him, however. It seemed as though Harden had put all his faith into Raven's capable, deadly hands and hadn't bothered coming up with a backup plan.

That worked in Clint's favor this time, allowing him to leave the Oriental Palace in a matter of seconds. After that short amount of time, he was back on the street and headed for Tam's hotel. Every step he took hurt Clint a little less as he forced himself to muscle his way through the wounds Raven had given him.

As he crossed the street and made his way to Tam's, Clint wondered if Raven had been using some of those Empty Hand techniques that Motega had been telling him about. The styles didn't look exactly similar, but then again, Clint didn't consider himself an expert on the subject either. Raven's speed and deadly fighting style had almost been enough to overcome Clint's gun. There was no doubt in Clint's mind that the next time he met Raven, the other man wouldn't let up on his assault until one of them was dead.

Although Clint knew better than to waste any time on his end either, he still wasn't looking forward to crossing paths with Raven in the near future. One more inhale followed by another stabbing pain in his side acted like a splash of cold water in Clint's face.

Suddenly, he wished he did see Raven somewhere close by. The intense pain grated on Clint's nerves, firing up his anger until he almost considered turning away from the hotel and tracking down Raven once and for all. That's when he saw the group of people huddled in the alley next to Tam's hotel.

Clint picked up his pace, preparing himself for the worst as he placed his hand over his Colt and searched for what could be causing the commotion. Since Raven could have been anywhere in the vicinity, he figured that was the source of the disturbance. But even Raven wasn't fast enough to kill three men in the short time since he'd left the Oriental Palace.

The bodies could be seen lined up on the ground just inside the alley. Even though they were covered with blankets, the shapes were unmistakable. Clint kept an eye out for Raven, even when he saw Tam walking out of the alley with his hands clasped in front of him.

"What happened?" Clint asked.

The Chinese man lowered his hands and quickly scanned the area around him. He then motioned for Clint to come closer before saying, "It seems that Motega's enemies already knew he was here. They sent an animal of a man after him."

Clint's muscles tensed and his hand closed around the grip of his gun. "Where is he?"

"He is gone."

"And Motega?"

Tam paused for a second. "He is nearby. I don't know where."

Clint could read the old man's face well enough to

know that he was lying because he felt uncomfortable with so many people around. At that moment, Clint couldn't exactly blame him.

"How many were hurt?" Clint asked, looking back toward the crowded alley.

"Three of my men are dead. The killer was hurt but escaped. See there for yourself."

Clint reflexively glanced in the direction that Tam was nodding. After what had happened in the Oriental Palace, he found himself anxious to end the fight that had started there. When he looked where Tam indicated, however, Clint found something else besides the face of a killer.

He saw Motega staring intently at him from across the street. As soon as Clint made eye contact, the Indian stepped back into a shadow and disappeared.

"Go now," Tam said, having already turned his eyes away from where Motega had been standing. "Find your enemy and stop him before more people are slaughtered. Do not ask me about Motega again. Sadly, I can no longer be of any assistance to him or you."

Clint understood the Chinese man's message perfectly well. Tam was afraid that someone was listening to him, which was why he pointed silently to Motega while saying out loud that he didn't know where the Indian could be.

Tam had no need to disguise the rest of his message. Whoever these enemies were, they needed to be found and stopped. Until that was done, Clint and Motega were on their own.

THIRTY-THREE

Taking a roundabout way that almost led him out of the Chinese section of town, Clint looped through back alleys and alternate streets before heading back to the spot where Motega was waiting. He was just about to cross over to that shadowy section when he caught a glimpse of movement from the corner of his eye.

What he saw was Elle standing on a corner. Her arms were wrapped around herself as protection from the cold and she was nervously shifting from one foot to another. As she rubbed her arms and stomped her feet, she studied the street around her, her search captivating every bit of her attention.

Clint worked his way up behind her without making more than a rustle of sound. When he tapped her on the shoulder, he thought she damn near jumped out of her skin.

Elle's body twitched, and she would have let out a startled yelp if Clint hadn't pressed his hand against her mouth just in time. She relaxed immediately when she saw him and stayed quiet when he took his hand away.

Already stepping back into the dark, Clint curled his finger back to motion for her to follow him. She took another quick glance around, stepped down from the boardwalk and then walked into the tight space between two neighboring buildings.

"I was looking for you," she said in a rush once she saw that Clint had stopped walking and was leaning against a wall. She walked up to Clint and wrapped her arms around him, squeezing him with all her strength. "I was so worried about you. I didn't know if that man found you or if you found him or what was going on."

Clint didn't embrace her, but draped one arm over her shoulders. He kept the other hand free to reach for his gun if the need came up. "You seem awfully concerned about a man you just met a few minutes ago."

She stepped back and nodded. "Sorry if I was too forward. It's just that I heard you were coming and was hoping you might be the one to put Mr. Harden in his place."

"You know who I am?"

Pausing for a moment, Elle nodded as though she wasn't sure if he was serious in asking the question. "Of course I know who you are. You're Clint Adams. You're The Gunsmith."

"And how did you know I was coming to town? Hell, I didn't even know I'd be coming until I was only a day's ride from here."

"Mr. Harden has scouts working for him. Folks from saloons and every hotel in town get something for reporting to him. He even pays children to let him know when they see something interesting. That way, he always has a good idea of what's going on in town."

"Simple but effective, I guess. Now, what is he doing that makes you want to see someone like me come in and take him down?"

"The man's a pig. He has killers working for him who have shot people down in the street. He doesn't even truly own the Palace. All he does is lay around, make threats and acts like a king. I hate him. Most everybody hates him."

"Then why doesn't anyone do anything about him?" Clint asked. "Doesn't this town have a sheriff?"

"We do, but he's away on business most of the time. Right now, he's overseeing a hanging two towns away."

"Then maybe some deputies need to be hired."

Elle stepped back and looked at Clint suspiciously. "Why are you asking so many questions? After what just happened, I would have thought you'd be anxious to give Mr. Harden some payback."

"I've got my own business to handle. I'm not a hired gun and I'm not here to step in for a lazy sheriff."

Nodding, Elle said, "That's fair, I suppose. But your business has to do with Mr. Harden, right? I mean, that's why you came here in the first place isn't it?"

"Yes it is." Glancing out of the alley, Clint couldn't find any sign that they'd been followed. Most of the activity in the street was still in the vicinity of the Oriental Palace and Tam's hotel. When he looked farther into the alley, Clint saw a subtle hint of motion that was Motega shifting in the shadows.

He could tell by looking at Elle's face that she had been genuinely concerned for him. Either that, or she was awfully good at leading men astray. Considering where she worked, that second option had a good deal of weight behind it.

"You could have been killed, you know," he said, watching her face carefully. "Didn't you think about that before charging down those stairs with a gun in your hand?"

"To be honest . . . I didn't."

At that moment, Clint could see fear seeping into her features. It drifted over her face like a shadow, leaving her chilled and shaking in its wake.

"All I knew was that Mr. Harden was in a different

room than the one you were taken to," she said. "I didn't know why, since I thought he wanted to talk to you, but then I heard Max say that you would never see the light of day."

She turned away from Clint and lowered her head. By the way she tightened her arms around herself and lifted her shoulders, it seemed as though Elle was feeling an even more powerful chill than the one already in the wintry air. "Nobody uses that room unless they want to do things that nobody else can hear. There's no other door leading into it. Not even the sheriff knows it's there. A girl can scream as loud as she wants and it doesn't even matter that the parlor is right on the other side of the wall. All that gets out is a peep and nobody can hear that through all the talking and piano playing.

"I hate that room. Bad things happen there. Girls get hurt or . . . or worse when someone pays enough to sleep there." Elle paused for a moment and stared at the ground with glassy eyes. "When Max lied to you and then made you go down into that room, I guess I just . . . I just acted without thinking. I knew something bad was going to happen."

Clint took her by the shoulders and slowly moved her around until she was facing him. He then lifted her face with a finger beneath her chin and stared into her eyes until he could tell she was truly staring back at him. After listening to everything she'd said and watching her while she spoke, Clint was convinced that she wasn't acting.

No actress could put on that much fear without giving herself away somehow. Besides that, he'd already uncovered enough facts on his own to back up what she'd been saying.

"You did a kind thing going back in there after me like that," he told her. "I truly thank you."

She smiled weakly and lifted a hand to brush against Clint's arm. "I was supposed to get close to you when you arrived. But when I saw you, I could tell there was something different about you. I could tell that you were a good man underneath it all."

"Really? Even after all the things you've heard about me?"

"Yes," she said with a smile. "In my line of work, I meet plenty of men, and some of them feel they can hurt a lady just because they paid for some of their time. It's important to be able to spot men like that. I felt safe when I was close to you, Clint. Just like I feel safe right now."

"Well, you're not safe. Neither of us is."

THIRTY-FOUR

"If you need somewhere to rest, there's a cabin on the eastern edge of town," Elle told him.

"That might not be a great idea," Clint said, more to himself then to her.

But Elle shook her head and added even more insistence to her voice. "It's all by itself and has a pump right next to the door. You'll know it when you see it. You can stay there for as long as you like. Everyone thinks it's deserted. Not even Mr. Harden knows about it."

"How'd you manage to keep that secret from him?"

"My family's lived here a hell of a lot longer than his sorry hide has been in town. Ever since my parents died, there hasn't been a soul in that place. Not even to take out the furniture. I kept it the way it was so I could stay there sometimes when I wanted to feel like I was away from this place. I'll bet most everyone else in town forgot it's even there."

After all that had happened, Clint was feeling jumpy over just about everything he saw or heard. For some reason, though, he didn't get any kind of uneasy feeling about anything Elle had been saying. Having come to a point where he trusted his own gut instincts more than just about everything else, Clint let himself follow their lead this time as well.

Nodding, he said, "I might just take you up on that."

"I really wish you would. If Mr. Harden is out for you, then there probably aren't many other safe places to sleep in town anyways."

"Thanks for the kindness. If I do need to use that place, I'll be sure to leave it just the way I found it."

"All right."

"You'd better get going now. Someone's bound to miss you before too long. Especially after the way you stuck your neck out for me earlier." Suddenly, Clint felt as though he didn't want to let her go running back to the Oriental Palace. "On second thought, maybe you should lay low for a bit, too."

"Don't worry about me, Clint. I can handle myself. Besides, the girls at the Palace won't let me walk into anything too dangerous. I swear they know what's going on around here better than anyone else."

"Well, you take care of yourself," Clint said, running a hand through her soft, flowing hair. "I owe you a favor, so don't let anything happen until you get a chance to collect."

Suddenly, Elle leaned forward and pressed her lips against Clint's. She held them there for a few seconds, until their body heat warmed both of them up. The warmth flowed from the kiss and spread throughout Clint's entire body, filling him with an excitement and sense of urgency that made him wish they were both alone in that cabin right then and there.

She must have felt that as well, because her body began to move in closer and writhe against him. Her breathing became quicker and more intense, while her hands reached up to slide around the back of Clint's neck. Elle let out a soft groan when she felt Clint's hands on her body, moving over her hips and up along her sides.

All Clint had to do was open his mouth slightly and he
felt the soft, moist touch of Elle's tongue on his lips. He
moved one hand over her back, so he could feel her hair
glide between his fingers, while his other hand stayed on
the gentle slope of her waist.

Even though they kissed for at least a minute or two,
it seemed to end all too quickly. Their lips broke contact,
but their faces remained close to one another. They stared
into each other's eyes for another few seconds before Elle
finally moved away.

"Be careful, Clint," she said. "I really hope to see you
again."

"Thanks again for your help."

She started to speak, but then held back the words before a single one of them could escape from her lips.
Instead, she nodded and turned to walk out of the alley.
After stepping back onto the boardwalk, she turned
around to look over her shoulder toward the alley.

All she saw was empty space and shadows.

Clint was nowhere to be found.

The moment Elle left the alley, Clint ducked back into
the darkness until he could feel the cold shadows wrapped
all the way around him. It felt as though the temperature
was dropping by the second, and his breath looked like
thick steam as it curled from his mouth and nose.

He didn't bother trying to look for Motega. Instead,
Clint simply kept walking as silently as he could so he
could avoid drawing any unwanted attention. When he
reached the back of the alley, he stopped before leaving
the confines of the close quarters.

"Be careful, friend," came a familiar voice from somewhere very close to where Clint was standing. "Mine are
not the only people who have tales about great warriors
being undone by a woman."

Following the sound of the voice, Clint looked up and

quickly picked out the solid form standing cloaked in shadow. "And I'm sure your people have something against eavesdropping, too. If they don't, I can tell you where to start."

Motega was grinning as he stepped out from his hiding spot so Clint could see him better. "I listened only so I could advise you. In troubled times, it is always better to have more than one man leading the way."

"I'll bet there are plenty of sewing circles out there that would just love that bit of advice." Clint managed to keep a straight face for a couple seconds before his sarcastic smile shone through. "The only smart piece of thinking I can come up with right now is to get ourselves out of the open so we can catch our breath."

Motega nodded once and said, "I have already scouted ahead. There is a place on the other end of town that seemed crowded enough for us to slip in and rest without being spotted right away."

"Just as long as we're away from the Chinese district, I'd say we'll be all right until word spreads about what happened. After that, we might have to come up with something else."

Pausing just a bit, Motega added, "Perhaps that dark-haired friend of yours has a friend she could steer my way."

"Now that's the kind of thinking I'm used to."

THIRTY-FIVE

As it turned out, both Clint and Motega were right in their thinking about finding another place where they could lay low for a bit. As soon as they had worked their way out of the Chinese section of Padre's Crossing, there were fewer people watching them and fewer still who were on the lookout for men fitting Clint and Motega's description.

The saloon that Motega picked as their destination was indeed stuffed to the rafters with people who all seemed to be too wrapped up in their own business to notice much of anything else. Motega walked in first and found a place to sit at a small table in the back of the room. Clint came in soon after, working his way up to the bar, where he ordered a beer before heading over to where Motega was waiting.

As he made his way through the room, Clint nearly lost sight of Motega several times. By the time he got to the proper table and pulled up a chair, Clint couldn't even see through the milling bodies to the front door. That made him a bit uncomfortable at first, but the tradeoff was that it was equally difficult to spot them inside the crowd.

At first, Clint thought he might have picked the wrong table. When he looked down at Motega without the Indian

being wrapped in shadows, he spotted the bruises and
dried blood on Motega's face.

"Jesus," Clint said as he sat down and set his mug upon
the table. "What the hell happened to you?"

"I was just about to ask you the same thing."

Hearing that, Clint's hand went reflexively up to the
sore spots on his face. The stab of pain he felt instantly
brought back mental pictures of his recent encounter in
the Oriental Palace. "Why don't we start with you? I'm
dying to know who could possibly do that much damage
to someone as quick on their feet as you."

Motega gave a short recount of his fight with Abe outside of Tam's hotel. When he did give details, they were
mostly concerning the way Abe fought. He spoke about
his own injuries as though they were inconsequential,
even though his face was swollen in several places and
his leather clothing was torn and bloodied.

When he was done, Motega waved to a server who was
walking back to the bar. He asked for water and was sure
to keep himself from looking directly into the worker's
face. Although the server was about to insist that the Indian buy something with alcohol in it, she got a look at
Motega and grudgingly agreed to bring some water.

Clint made things right in the server's mind by ordering
another beer for himself and sent her on her way before
she could concern herself too much with the pair.

"So he was waiting for you?" Clint asked after the
server returned with the drinks.

Nodding, Motega said, "I'd say he knew where to look.
By the looks of him, he was going to kick down Tam's
door if I hadn't already come outside on my own."

"So Tam's place wasn't as safe as you thought." Clint
took a sip of beer. Although he hated to say it, he couldn't
let the next question go unspoken. "Do you think Tam or
one of his men sold you out?"

"If that was Tam's doing, he would not have sent three

of his own men to their deaths trying to help me in the fight. That animal killed them without a thought." Motega took a sip of water and winced as the cold liquid ran down his throat. "If anything, Tam's only mistake was in not knowing that his secret had been discovered. Someone knew about him and the help he offers to those in need. That is the betrayer we seek."

"Who does Tam help?" Clint asked. "No offense, but I didn't see too many faces like mine when I was in there."

"He helps those he can trust. Unfortunately, he does not trust the white man. You are right in thinking his kindness does not extend to everyone in need. In fact, there are very few that I know of who actually know who Tam is or what he does."

"So that means whoever tipped off this crazy man that came after you today used to be in Tam's good graces."

"Yes. That would have to be true." In a way, admitting that seemed to hurt Motega more than the wounds his body had suffered. After reflecting on that for a short while, the Indian looked back at Clint and said, "Now tell me about what happened to you. It seems as though you might have been almost as occupied as I was."

Clint polished off the rest of one beer and half of the second as he told Motega about what had happened when he went to the Oriental Palace. As he spoke about the fighting style that had been used against him, Clint watched Motega's face for any changes or reaction. There was plenty to be seen and Motega didn't appear to be trying to hide one bit of it.

"And this man you fought," Motega said, weighing every word as though each was just as important as the others. "Was he a bit shorter than me with dark eyes and long black hair?"

Clint nodded. So far, he'd purposely left out the name

of the man who'd attacked him. "Yes. He looked pretty much like that."

"And his skin was a bit lighter than mine. Not quite Chinese in appearance, but not quite similar to me, either."

"Right on both counts. You know him, don't you?"

"His name is Raven, and yes, I do know him. Did he tell you as much?"

"It's not exactly like he had to," Clint said before taking another drink of beer. "He moved and fought close enough to your style that I figured it couldn't have been a coincidence. From what he was saying, it sounded like he'd been following us both ever since we met up."

"That is his way," Motega said. "He will circle over the heads of his enemies and pluck out their eyes when he feels they are at their weakest."

Clint shook his head and let out a single, humorless laugh. "Great. That's just great. Does he know about Tam's hotel?"

"Yes."

"At least that answers that question. So tell me about this Raven. When you say he plucks out his enemy's eyes, that's just an exaggeration, right?"

Motega looked up and met Clint's stare. He didn't shake or nod his head. He didn't say a word.

"Great," Clint said again. "That's just great."

THIRTY-SIX

"Raven walked the path set down by Master Po well before I lost my father," Motega said. "He was called by his true name back then and was one of Master Po's finest pupils."

"That's until you came along, though, right?" Clint asked, thinking he knew where the Indian's story was going.

Motega shook his head. "The way of the Empty Hand does not work like that. If you practiced drawing your pistol for ten years, would you expect someone to be quicker than you after doing the same for less than half the time?"

"No. I guess I wouldn't."

"Master Po had several students, but they were left behind when he left his country and again when he was able to leave his enslavement. Raven was with him ever since he was a boy, and Master Po had taken responsibility for him after Raven's parents were taken to the Spirit World.

"Master Po began his teachings early in Raven's life and continued them throughout their years together. I was only accepted as a student after Raven was well on his way down the path." Motega drifted off for a moment,

his eyes wandering away from Clint and into pictures
from the past shown to him by his mind.

Before too long, the Indian shook himself back into the
present and took a drink of water. "Master Po looked on
Raven as a son, just as Raven looked on me as a brother.
We had no home, but we were as one family. Master Po
was the house under which we both found shelter."

"That all sounds fine and good," Clint said. "But why
can't you even speak your brother's name? I know families have their spats, but that sounds like a bit much to
me."

Motega took a breath and dabbed his finger into his
water. He then rubbed the water onto his face and again
onto the wound in his side. "Are you familiar with the
ways of my people?"

"I've known some Indians in my day and we usually
find some common ground. I've seen some of their dances
and rituals, but I'm no expert."

"My father used to pass on stories about his tribe and
their ancient histories. We believe in animal spirits which
can help us or hurt us, much like your god and angels.

"Some of these spirits aren't good or evil, but merely
troublesome. They toy with mortal men as only a spirit
can. We call these spirits tricksters, and there are as many
humorous tales regarding them as there are those filled
with darkness and terror. Hare is a trickster. So is Coyote.
One of the most powerful of them is Raven.

"A trickster plants seeds of chaos and disorder. He top-
ples what man has built to show him his weakness. But
the tricksters are most dangerous when they do what they
do for no other reason than their own amusement."

"And this fellow student," Clint said, "this brother of
yours was named for one of these tricksters? Is that a good
thing or bad?"

"At one point in my travels with Master Po, the white
man wanted nothing more than to capture my teacher. The

sheriffs and Army said he was responsible for killing a railroad crew so he could escape."

Clint was wrapped up in Motega's story so much that he could almost picture the old Chinese man, even though he'd never laid eyes on Po. "Is that true?" he asked.

"My master has killed when there was no other alternative, and he did work on the crew where those men worked. But Master Po never killed like that. Those railroad workers were slaughtered like animals. They were torn apart and left to rot.

"They were killed after Master Po and I had gone, but no white man wanted to hear that. They thought my teacher was old and easy prey, so they would have no trouble finding him and forgetting about the rest. Nobody questioned why an old man would want to kill seven men when he could just walk away in the night so much easier."

Motega paused to take a drink. As he thought back to the story he was telling, he lifted the cup back to his mouth and drained the rest of the water in a few swallows. That seemed to give him the energy to move on and relive that night through his own words.

"When Master Po was accused of this crime, a price was put on his head," Motega continued. "He had to head out and keep moving, without even stopping once in a town or settlement. He had to be ready to move at a moment's notice if the law happened to cross his path.

"Even with all of this, he still wanted to take one of us with him. I was traveling at his side, but my brother was nearby. Master Po could not travel with us both, so he chose me to accompany him. But my brother would not leave us behind. He followed us and would help when he could."

"Help?" Clint said after sipping his beer. "What do you mean?"

"He would travel with us, but at a distance. Sometimes

he would move ahead and scout our way. If he found trouble further along our path, he would take care of it for us." Motega smiled fondly as the memories flowed through him. "We would find men who looked like they were asleep. Lawmen and even small cavalry groups. They were not asleep, though. Some were knocked out. Some were dead."

"How did you know who was doing it?"

"Can you tell what kind of gun killed another by examining the wound?" Motega asked.

"To some degree, I guess."

"It is the same with the way of the Empty Hand. A man's fighting style is as distinctive as the face he wears or the eyes in his head. I was almost certain my spirit brother was doing these things. Master Po knew without a doubt.

"I was younger then. I saw those bodies as a blessing. I thought my brother in spirit was haunting us. Protecting us. He would leave things like food or supplies, just like the friendly tricksters in my father's stories. For that and because I could never see him, I began calling him Raven."

Clint had been watching Motega carefully. Not only did he find the story interesting, but he never thought he'd see the Indian talk for so long in one sitting. He knew it would have been foolish not to take advantage of his openness while it lasted.

"This sounds like a good story," Clint said. "But when you talk about him, there seems to be something you don't like thinking about." Clint's hand drifted up to one of the bruised welts on his face. "And that sure as hell doesn't sound like the guy who gave me these."

"Master Po did not find Raven's antics amusing," Motega went on. "Much like the stories of my ancestors, he saw the trickster as something of a curse. He would say prayers over the bodies that were left behind, even if they were men that would have shot us on sight. He would not take the supplies left for us and would not even let Raven's food pass his lips.

"I asked him what was wrong and why he wasn't thankful for the help Raven was giving us." Once again, Motega flinched slightly as though the thoughts within his head were physically hurting him. He choked back the pain and said, "Master Po told me that Raven was doing his favors to us because of a guilty conscience.

"You see, Clint, I never saw the bodies of those men at the railroad camp. Master Po did. He described them to me and I thought he was describing the bodies that we would find along the trail next to the supplies and food left for us."

"Jesus Christ," Clint whispered.

"Raven killed those men at that camp. And not too long after Master Po told me these things, Raven began trying to kill us as well."

THIRTY-SEVEN

"Why?" Clint asked after Motega said the words that seemed to hit him harder than any fist. "Why would he want to kill you or your teacher?"

"Raven spoke to us one last time, at Master Po's request. My master told him that he would have no part of someone who would take life so recklessly. He said that Raven squandered the gift of his teachings and that he was no longer welcome in his presence.

"He turned his back on him then," Motega said. "Master Po literally turned his back on Raven and walked away. After that, Raven looked at me and I could see that there was a fire burning beneath his tears and pain. He hated me from that day onward. Beyond that, who can say why a killer does the things he does?"

Clint nodded, thinking back to all the killers he'd met in his lifetime. Sometimes it helped to know why they acted the way they did, but that usually didn't change much. Whether or not he knew the purpose behind a murderer's actions, that didn't bring any of his victims back to life. Sometimes, Clint wished he didn't know what went on inside those dark minds. It was much easier to believe in a happy world without knowing things like that.

"I now understand why those four men never came after us when we were headed into town," Motega said. "Something seemed familiar about their absence. When those men that were chasing me seemed to disappear after a while, it was almost as though the trickster was watching over me once again. Now I know that was exactly what was happening."

"But if Raven wants you and your teacher dead, why would he do anything to protect you?"

The Indian shrugged and wrapped his hands around the cup which had been cooled by the water he'd drunk. "If he was following us, I know those four men are dead. What use is it to try and guess why they died? The tricksters are so dangerous because they are unpredictable. Raven does as he wishes. The reasons are his own."

With that, the Indian seemed to have run out of steam. He stared down into his cup as though the world around him had just faded away. His breathing was becoming slower and more shallow due in no small part to effort on his part.

Clint knew they didn't have a whole lot of time to kick back and relax, even though they did seem to have gone completely unnoticed inside the crowded saloon. He wanted to get moving once again, before someone came along who worked for Mr. Harden or had gotten word from some of the wrong people. Surely it wouldn't be long before the scouts Elle had warned him about made their way into the crowd that Clint was using for protection.

In fact, for all he knew, Elle was one of those scouts. He didn't get that feeling from her, but he was only human and had been known to err from time to time. But he could also tell that Motega needed a minute to pull himself through the turmoil that was boiling inside of him.

The longer he watched, the more Clint could see the change coming over the Indian's face. The differences were subtle, but they were easy enough to spot if one knew what to look for. Within a minute or two, the air near Motega lost some of the tension that had crackled around him as though a storm was about to break.

Finally, Motega let out a sigh and blinked. "Knowing who we face is helpful. Unfortunately, I don't know about the one man who chose me as his target this night."

"You mean that big redheaded bastard who refused to feel a drop of pain?"

"That's the one. There are places to hit someone that deadens their limbs or stops their heart. I can even make it difficult for them to draw a breath. I struck that man in every one of those areas, but he felt nothing. It was like I was hitting a brick wall."

"And you couldn't even get him to drop his gun?"

Motega shook his head. "He shouldn't have been able to make a fist, but he never let go of that pistol. It might have been sewn to his palm for all I know."

"Well, I say our first priority is to get some rest and try to heal up."

"There is no time for rest," Motega insisted. "Master Po could be wounded as we speak. He may have been taken somewhere."

"A lot of things could have happened, but we will most definitely lose this fight if we try to limp in there before we're ready." Clint waited until he saw that his words had gotten through. "This isn't over, Motega. Not by a long shot. Would your teacher think it smart to run when you're almost too tired to walk?"

Surprisingly enough, the Indian actually smiled at that. "No, he would not. That actually sounds like the exact words he might have said if he were in your position."

"Then he really must be a smart man."

Both of them cracked smiles after Clint said that, and laughter was soon to follow. Having the mood lightened did them both some good, but even laughing sent ripples of pain through Clint from several places in his aching body.

"Do you know somewhere else that might be safe?" Clint asked. "Somewhere you can rest that Raven wouldn't know about?"

After taking a moment to think it over, Motega nodded. "Perhaps. What about you?"

"I think it might be better if we found separate places to hole up for the night. Once word gets around that Harden is after us, folks will be looking for two people. We can blend in a little easier by ourselves, and that way we only have to watch our own backs for a bit."

"Then we should meet up somewhere after we wake?"

"Yeah. You know this town better than I do. Any suggestions?"

"The corner of Third and Oak. It is usually busy there throughout the day, and it isn't far from most anywhere in town." After a slight pause, Motega added, "And Clint. If you want to take this opportunity to rid yourself of this situation, I understand. You didn't ask for this fight."

"Neither did you. I'll look for you at that corner around eight in the morning, so don't worry about me. I'm used to getting myself wrapped up in messes like this. My only problem is that I prefer to see them through."

Motega nodded. "Thank you, my friend. I vow to make sure you don't regret that choice."

"Sounds good. I think we should get out of this place and get some rest. Something tells me that tomorrow won't be any easier than today."

THIRTY-EIGHT

Motega got up and left the saloon first. Clint stuck around to pay for his drinks and find his way out of the saloon without appearing to be in a rush. When he stepped out of the crowded building and into the cold night, he couldn't see the first trace of the Indian.

There were no figures moving on the street. There wasn't even a set of tracks in the freshly fallen snow. Since he hadn't been expecting to spot Motega, Clint flipped up the collar of his jacket to keep the wind off his neck and headed for the end of town where Elle told him her cabin was waiting.

Along the way, he debated whether or not he should trust the brunette. The only decision he could come to before he got to the cabin was that he needed to rest and that her offer was as good as any other choice. Clint didn't know if Harden had any scouts in place or if he owned any of the other hotels in town, and he didn't have the time to find out.

If Elle was setting another trap for him, then Clint was of the mind to spring it and get it over with. Besides, it seemed that if she wanted to harm him, it would have been a hell of a lot easier to stand back and let Raven do the dirty work.

Clint kept to the streets that either had no lights or were left dark by winds strong enough to snuff out the lanterns. Elle's directions had been fairly simple, and it took him no time at all to spot the cabin all by itself with the pump out front. There was a dim light flickering behind one of the small windows, but no smoke coming from its chimney.

Stopping toward the end of the boardwalk, Clint hung back and waited beneath the overhang of the roof of the last storefront in the row. He shoved his hands into his pockets and let the night settle in around him, acquainting himself with the flow of the wind and the howl of the breezes that kicked the snowflakes this way and that.

There were voices in the distance, but those came from behind him. Every now and then, he could hear footsteps crunching in the snow and clomping over the boards, but those weren't coming from the direction of the cabin either. Those sounds all faded away before they got too close, however, convincing Clint that he wasn't about to be ambushed.

Of course, an ambush might be launched as soon as he got a little closer. Some attackers could already be waiting for him, entrenched in their spots and sighting down their rifles at that very moment.

"Aw, the hell with it," Clint grunted to himself. With that, he stepped down from the boardwalk and made his way to the cabin's front door.

The cabin itself was only big enough to have two normal sized rooms. Any more than that, and they would have been very close quarters indeed. It looked as though there had been a shingle with writing on it nailed next to the door at one time, but all that was left was a few nails through a broken strip of wood.

So far, Clint didn't get that instinctual feeling of danger

that sometimes let him know if things just weren't right. As if he needed more reasons to open the door, Clint started to feel some of the warmth coming through from the other side.

He waited there for a moment, listening for any sounds that might be coming from inside the structure. Hearing none, Clint grabbed the handle, opened the door, and stepped into the cabin.

The door opened onto a large room that was half kitchen and half sitting area. An old black stove sat right in the middle of the room, facing the table and cabinets that made up a little kitchen. On the other side of the stove was a large chair covered in a dusty blanket, as well as a few smaller chairs situated in a circle around a little circular table.

Clint looked around and noticed several other things about the place that made it seem as though the cabin had been abandoned in a hurry. There was a book laying open on the small round table, and there were even a few coats and an apron hanging from a row of hooks by the door.

The only thing that made it feel like Clint wasn't walking into an inhabited home was the layer of dust that had fallen over everything in sight. From the tops of the tables to the clothing hanging on the wall, the dust covered everything so completely that Clint felt as though he was seeing things in a shade of gray.

He knew he wasn't the only person to step through that door recently, however, mainly because of the two lit lanterns that were placed at both ends of the room. As he walked through the room, Clint also noticed that the top of the stove had been wiped clean.

"Hello?" came a tentative voice from another part of the cabin.

Clint turned on his heels as his hand dropped reflexively to his holster. It was then that he spotted a narrow doorway leading into the cabin's second room. And it was from there that the voice had come.

Keeping his eyes on that door and his ears open for any other suspicious sounds, Clint walked toward what appeared to be a little bedroom. "Hello," he answered. "Who's there?"

The other room was dark, but enough light was getting through from the lanterns to reflect on a brass bed frame. Reflected in the metal surface, a figure moved through the darkness and toward the door.

Clint was ready to draw in a heartbeat, but he kept the Colt in its place until he was certain there was danger.

The figure moved into the doorway. At first, all Clint could see was a slender outline clothed in pale white. Next, he saw the flowing dark hair, which was enough for him to take his hand away from his gun.

"I didn't mean to startle you," Elle said. "But you came in so quietly that I hardly even knew you were here."

Clint could tell she was nervously watching his gun hand. "Sorry about that, but I tend to get tense after already being ambushed once today."

"Mr. Harden was too busy talking to those animals he hired to notice much else. I left the Palace and came to make sure there was some food for you once you arrived. Then I found that I didn't want to leave without seeing you."

Not only could Clint start to pick up on the smell of the food Elle had mentioned, but he caught the scent of her as well. At that moment, he didn't want her to leave, either.

THIRTY-NINE

Elle was dressed in a creamy white nightgown that hung slightly off her shoulders and came down to just below her ankles. The color of the material made her skin seem soft and almost ghostly in the dim light. Her long black hair was slightly rumpled, as though it had been caught by a wayward breeze and then dropped back down again. She looked anything but disheveled, however, as she walked slowly from the bedroom.

"If you want me to leave, I will," she said softly. Her eyes were cast downward, as though she wasn't much looking forward to Clint's answer.

The scent that kept Clint's attention wasn't from her perfume. Although there was some of that sweetness mixed in, he was more stricken by the fresh scent of her skin and hair. It reminded him of the cool wind that blew after a heavy snow.

It was the fresh smell of pure comfort and quiet cold.

"Don't go," Clint said before he had a chance to re-phrase the sentiment in his mind. "I mean, this is your cabin, so it's not my place to say if you stay or leave."

Picking up on how she was affecting him, Elle moved a little closer while clasping her hands in front of her. "Is that all? And here I thought you might enjoy some company."

"I could say I prefer to be alone, but I'm sure you'd see right through that. Besides, I'm afraid you might take that food with you. Whatever it is, it smells great."

"There's just some chicken sandwiches and fruit from my cellar. It's not much but—"

"No," Clint interrupted. "It's a lot more than you needed to bring. Thanks a lot, Elle."

Her cheeks flushed slightly when she heard him say her name. She picked up her pace as she walked around him and went to a basket that had been sitting next to the stove. "I started to light a fire in here, but then I thought someone might see the smoke. It should be all right now since it's dark out."

"Yeah, it should be all right. Besides," Clint added with a grin, "anyone watching this place would have already seen the lanterns through the windows."

Elle stopped right where she was, and her eyes darted anxiously between the pair of lanterns burning on either side of the room. She frowned and started to walk toward the closest lantern. "I don't believe how stupid I am," she said in frustration.

She started to reach out for the lantern that was hanging on the wall in the kitchen, but was stopped when Clint took hold of her wrist. The grip was strong enough to keep her from moving, but not powerful enough to cause her any pain.

"Don't worry about that," Clint said. "Whatever is going to happen is going to happen. Leave the lantern lit and let's have a bite to eat."

"But what if someone sees?"

"Then they'll come. You're here already and so am I. You and I walking out of here will just attract more attention. Besides, if I was any more prepared for someone to find me, I'd be a nervous wreck."

Elle smiled, not so much because of what Clint said, but because of the sarcastic way in which he said it. Her lips seemed especially full and red so close to the flickering lantern, and Clint was too tired to resist them any longer.

All he had to do was move slightly toward her before Elle closed the rest of the distance on her own. They kissed as though they hadn't quite finished the last time their lips had touched, and the fire inside of them was instantly rekindled. Their breath went from one mouth straight into the other, warming Clint and Elle the way no fire could ever hope to do.

As Clint kissed her, he let his hands wander over her body, feeling the enticing curve of her hips through the soft cotton of her nightgown. She moved a little within his grasp, letting a soft moan slip out from the back of her throat and directly onto Clint's lips.

Just like a fire that had never been put all the way out, the heat between them rose even more as they lingered so close together. Soon, their bodies were pressing tight against one another and Clint was feeling his own reaction to the slow grinding motion of Elle against him.

The longer they kissed, the more Clint felt as though Elle's nightgown wasn't even there. She moved slowly back and forth within the soft material, sliding one leg up and down over Clint's thigh. His hands traced over her backside and up along her spine, feeling the smooth softness of her skin through the cotton.

It quickly became obvious to him that Elle wasn't wearing anything beneath her nightgown. He could feel nothing else except for the single layer of soft cotton between his hand and her naked body. Suddenly, Clint began to feel much different from how he'd felt only a second ago.

Whereas before it had seemed as though the nightgown was barely there, it now seemed as if the fabric was a barrier between him and what he wanted. He could still feel her through the material, but it frustrated him that he couldn't touch her flesh directly.

He wanted his hands on her skin, and Clint could think of nothing else at that moment in time.

As if sensing the turmoil that was building up inside of him, Elle wrapped her leg around him a little tighter and then slid it farther, up to his hip. Her knee bumped against his gunbelt, so she stopped there and pushed her hips straight forward until she could feel the bulge in his crotch. Locking her hands around the back of his neck the way she'd done earlier, Elle looked directly into Clint's eyes and let a smile glide slowly across her face.

"Is this why you came here, Clint Adams?" she asked, after pulling her lips away from his.

"No," Clint responded. "But I think this is why you stayed."

FORTY

Hearing him cut straight to the heart of the matter allowed Elle to put herself fully into his embrace. She let out a soft moan and leaned her head back so that Clint could begin passionately kissing her neck and shoulders.

He reached down with both hands to cup her buttocks, lifting her off the floor until she hopped up and wrapped her other leg around him. Still kissing and nibbling her neck, Clint carried her into the next room. His hands had bunched up a good portion of her nightgown until he could feel bare skin with his fingertips. That made his erection so hard that he felt the strain of still being in his clothing.

As soon as Elle was set down on the edge of her bed, she reached to unbuckle Clint's gunbelt and then his pants. One after another, his clothes fell to the floor until all she had to do was pull off his jacket and shirt. She tore at his clothes with growing intensity, sending several buttons flying through the air in the process.

In less than a minute, Clint was naked on top of her, crawling over her body and exploring the contours of her figure with both hands. She wriggled and squirmed beneath him, playfully shifting whenever she felt his touch drift too close to where he wanted to go.

Finally, Clint sat upright and straddled her waist. "All right," he said sternly. "You move way too much."

Before she could answer, Clint dropped down so that he pinned her by the wrists. Elle kept her eyes locked on him as she struggled halfheartedly beneath his weight. Clint took his time in lowering his face down to hers until he was close enough to feel her breath on his mouth.

"What are you going to do to me?" she whispered.

Now Clint was the one to smile, as he brushed his lips over hers. Just when he seemed about to say something, he took her upper lip between his teeth and gently nibbled back and forth. He watched as her eyes closed and her body relaxed under him. Clint moved the tip of his tongue over her lips, tracing a line down along her neck.

He barely had to put any pressure on her wrists to keep her down. On the contrary, Elle seemed to enjoy having him dominate her and didn't resist him in the least. She arched her back as she felt his tongue slide down past her neck and over the collar of her nightgown.

The smooth material slipped over her body as Clint ground on top of her. Taking the upper edge of the fabric between his teeth, he pulled it down until he could taste where the slope of her breasts began. Her breathing became heavy before it turned into a series of moans which built in intensity until they caused her chest to rise and fall. Now it seemed that Elle was feeling the same frustration that Clint had experienced earlier. She struggled more against the restraint of her clothing than against the weight of his body.

After he'd let her suffer long enough, Clint lifted himself up and pulled the nightgown over her head. The garment slid away from her body, leaving her stretched out on the bed with her arms extended over her head.

"That's better," she whispered without opening her

eyes. The smile on her face grew as Clint slid his hands over her bare flesh.

He started at her arms and brushed his fingers all the way down to her ribs. From there, he continued down to her hips and then grazed his palms over her outer thighs. Clint closed his fingers around her ankles, tightened them, and then worked his way back up.

Elle lay as still as she could, allowing him to move her as he saw fit and savoring the way Clint took his time exploring her body. At times, she would shudder in anticipation of where he would touch her next. And when he did touch her in those spots, she let out a deep, satisfied groan.

As Clint massaged her, he moved her legs apart and settled in between them. As his hands moved up over her stomach, he positioned his rigid penis against the wet lips of her vagina. Closing his hands around her breasts, he shifted his hips forward so the tip of his cock slid inside of her, and he could immediately feel her muscles tighten in response to the pleasure she experienced.

Once his hands had traveled all the way up her arms and had closed once again around her wrists, Clint moved his hips forward until he was buried inside of her. She spread her legs open so he could thrust all the way forward, arching her back as she took in every last inch.

She started to say something, but a breathy moan was all she could manage. Clint began slowly pumping in and out of her. Lowering himself slightly, he could feel her erect nipples brushing against his chest as he moved back and forth again and again.

When Elle moved her hands, Clint allowed her to escape his grasp. She slid her fingers through Clint's hair before pulling his face down close enough for her to kiss it. Starting with his lips, she kissed him insistently and worked her way down to his neck.

He thrust into her harder then, causing her to wrap her

arms tighter around him and bite his shoulder with building passion. Their bodies had begun to learn each other's
rhythm, moving together to make the pleasure they were
feeling even more powerful.

As the first hot traces of her climax worked their way
through her body, Elle let go of Clint and dropped back
against the bed. She gathered fistfuls of the blanket and
turned her head so she could let out a loud moan into the
soft, thick comforter.

Knowing that they couldn't make too much noise made
Clint want to cry out even more. Where he might normally have just enjoyed hearing the sound of Elle's voice,
he found that he wanted nothing more than to make some
of his own. But they did have to keep quiet, and even
though it was difficult doing so, it made the approaching
orgasm even more intense.

Clint felt the explosion welling up quickly inside of him
as his thrusts became more and more urgent. Sliding all
the way out of her, he let the tip of his cock touch against
her wet opening before plunging all the way in one last
time.

He felt her wet lips caress every inch of him until he
was buried inside of her. When he pushed in as far as he
could go, he arched his back and let his climax overpower
him. He slid out and pumped in once more, which was
all it took to send the shiver of ecstasy through Elle as
well.

They lay there for a few moments afterward, watching
the way the flicker of light from the other room played
over their naked skin.

FORTY-ONE

Although he'd let his eyes close a few times throughout the night, and even let his head touch the pillow once or twice, Clint didn't really get a bit of sleep before the sun's rays started to show in the sky. Too much had been happening, and there was too much yet to come, for him to relax enough to nod off.

Elle had brought food sufficient to fill his stomach with enough left over to give them both a small breakfast. They started a fire in the stove just to brew coffee before quickly snuffing the flames. That heated the water as well as a small part of the kitchen, and they both enjoyed the warmth as well as each other's company.

Every so often, Clint would take a look through the windows, but he never did find any trace of someone approaching the cabin. It seemed that the rest of the town truly didn't know about the place and left it alone. By the time they were finishing their coffee, Clint felt a little guilty for keeping one suspicious eye on Elle for a good part of his stay in the cabin.

While sipping their coffee and watching the sunrise, Clint and Elle didn't say more than two words to each other. Instead, she leaned her head on his shoulder and enjoyed the simple, quiet moment. Clint had to admit that being there in the first minutes of that new day made him feel more rested than any amount of sleep.

"How are you feeling?" Elle asked once the sun had broken over the horizon. Her eyes moved over Clint's face and the blood that had soaked into his shirt.

Clint stretched out his arms and rolled his head to work some of the kinks from his neck. "Actually, there's still some pain in just about every part of my body." Clint hadn't told Elle about everything that was going on, or who Motega and Raven were. He figured that would give her less to worry about.

"I didn't make you feel any better last night?"

"To be honest, I'm surprised I was able to move that well at all. It just goes to show what a little real inspiration will do for a man."

She smiled, but still couldn't hide the fact that there was something bothering her. "I don't want you to go back there, Clint. I don't know what Mr. Harden is planning or why he wants to kill you so badly, but it would just be better for you to leave now while there's still a chance."

"There're lives at stake," Clint said plainly. "I can't just turn my back on that. Plus, I still haven't had my meeting with Harden. He owes me a few moments of his time."

"And am I supposed to just let you go, knowing what I know about Mr. Harden? I've seen the killers he has on his payroll and I've heard about the things that have happened to folks who have crossed him. It wasn't until I met you that I actually saw someone who Mr. Harden was going to hurt."

"It's not so easy to let things go when you know that the victim is a real person who walks and talks, is it?" Clint asked.

"I would hear people talk about Mr. Harden or the things he'd done or the guns he'd hired and it all seemed . . . exciting." Admitting that made Elle turn her eyes away from Clint. "I would hear about the bodies that were buried or the people who'd disappeared. But when I saw you and then realized something was going to happen, it seemed different.

"I couldn't just shake your hand and talk to you before pointing you toward someone who wanted to kill you. I've never been involved in things like that. Not directly."

"And you did a good thing," Clint said. "But now you know why I just can't leave before this is done. There is someone else who might get hurt if I don't lend a hand. He might already be hurt. Even if he's already dead, that will just mean Harden will move on to someone else. If I don't do something here and now, I'll be a little responsible for all the others that die by Harden's orders. Do you understand that?"

Elle nodded. "Yes. I understand. But that doesn't mean I have to like it. I'm more concerned with keeping you safe. You're the first person I've ever helped like that. If you get yourself killed now, you'll take that away from me."

"Tell you what. I'll just make sure that I come out of this alive. That way, we both get what we want. How's that sound?"

Although her smile was weak, it was still heartfelt. "If that's the best I can get, I guess I'll take it."

"Thanks for everything, Elle."

"Just don't forget about that deal you made. Promise me you'll take care of yourself."

"I promise."

They kissed slowly at first, but then let their passions build until Clint forced himself to pull back. He waved to Elle and then left the cabin.

FORTY-TWO

The earth was cold and hard beneath Clint's feet. Walking toward the spot where he was to meet Motega, Clint noticed how the ground felt as though the dirt had been replaced with rock overnight. The temperature had dropped so much that everything without a pulse had frozen solid.

The sun was shining brightly, which added a little warmth, but not nearly enough to make Clint's blood feel like anything but chilled river water. It helped to keep his steps lively and his hands shoved deep into his jacket pockets. Clint made it to the corner of Third and Oak in no time at all, and he quickly realized why Motega had picked that spot.

It seemed as though every person in town was out and walking around that particular area. Between the shops and restaurants, the boardwalk was rattling with all the feet pounding over it, and the street was filled with horses and carriages passing within inches of each other.

Clint stepped up to the edge of the boardwalk, where he could stand on the verge of all the activity. He stood there and watched the locals pass by, hoping that Motega would find him before he had to wade into all that madness.

As if answering the mental request, a tap came on Clint's shoulder, followed by a low voice.

"Did anyone find you?"

Clint turned to see the Indian standing beside him. "If they did, they were sure quiet about it. What about you?"

"My night was quiet as well. I did get a chance to do some scouting." Motega glanced around just to make sure that nobody was close enough to overhear him. "Master Po is here. I saw him being taken to the jail."

"I guess the sheriff left his keys in the wrong hands while he was away. How about we go get them?"

"You waste no time, friend. There are a few of them at the jail, but most of them are back at that whorehouse in the Chinese district. Where should we go first?"

"I'm here to help you," Clint said. "We can hit the leaders at the Palace first, but they might send someone to kill your teacher if we're not quick about it. They might be ready for us at the jail, but it's tough to say if we can handle springing another one of those traps."

"It would be foolish for us to split up again, but it may be our best chance of covering all the possibilities." Motega shook his head slowly and began walking along the side of the street. "There is no easy way, I'm afraid."

Falling into step next to the Indian, Clint said, "I'll go have my chat with Harden. That's as good a place to start as any."

"But he will surely be under guard. And if Raven is working with him, then there could be any number of dangers awaiting us."

"That's why we have to be more prepared than the last time we tried this. Even though it was painful, we both learned a hell of a lot about the men we're up against. I think I see a simple way to tip the balance back in our favor, at least for a little while."

"A little may not be enough."

Clint nodded. "This is going to be like walking into a powderkeg with a lit match in our hand. Things are going to get real hot really fast, and the same strategy for surviving that powderkeg will see us both through this explosion as well."

"What strategy is that?"

"When the fuse is lit, we need to run like hell."

Motega stopped in his tracks and turned to look Clint straight in the eye. Judging by the expression on his face, the Indian was not at all happy with Clint's suggestions. "I will not run, Clint. I would rather die first."

"And what were you doing when I first found you?" Clint asked.

His eyes narrowing, Motega said, "That was different. I was leading them to ground more suited for a fight I could win. I was not running away."

"This will be different, too. It will be different for exactly the same reason. Yesterday, we both almost got skinned alive because we were caught unprepared for what was thrown at us. We know what's out there now, but that redhead and your brother think all they need to do is finish us off. And if we go after them in the same way, they might do just that."

"So you suggest we run away?"

"No. I'm suggesting we run like hell. The most important thing is that we make sure they follow."

From there, Clint spelled out the rest of the plan he'd been kicking around in his head since early that morning. At first, Motega still didn't approve. But the Indian let Clint say his piece, and before too long he was beginning to warm up to what Clint had in mind.

They were at the end of Third Street by the time Clint had finished. The crowd wasn't as thick as before, but they were no longer in need of the cover it had provided. The Oriental Palace was straight ahead and to the right, while the jail was straight ahead and to the left. All they needed to do was decide which way they were going to go.

"So what do you say?" Clint asked. "You like my plan, or did you have something better in mind? You know Raven better than I do, so you tell me if this has a chance of working out."

"It has a chance, Clint," Motega replied with admiration. "The chance may not be as large as I would have hoped for, but it is a good chance all the same. Master Po would be proud of both of us if we survive. But you are right in saying that we don't have much time to follow through."

"Then we'll just have to hit hard and be quick about it."

"Yes," Motega said solemnly. "You are right about that."

"Glad to see you have so much confidence in me."

The Indian held out a hand, which Clint took in his grasp. "You are a fine warrior, Clint Adams. My father would have counted you among his friends."

"Then let's do him proud."

They turned and broke away from each other. Clint turned right and Motega went left.

FORTY-THREE

"You're not going to believe this," Max said as he stared out the window on the second floor of the Oriental Palace.

Harden was at his desk, casually going over some figures written in one of his bank books. "I'm not in the mood for guessing games, Max. Spit it out."

"It's Clint Adams. He's walking through the front door right now."

Dropping the pencil he'd been holding, Harden jumped to his feet. "I don't believe it. Where's Henry and the others?"

"In one of the rooms, sir. I believe they're, uh, indisposed at the moment."

"Well, tell them to pull their britches on and get downstairs now! And what about that other fellow? The one who let Adams go yesterday."

"I'm right here." Raven was standing at the door with his hands hanging down at his sides. He stood like a statue carved from granite, with both eyes burning within their sockets. "I just came here to make sure you keep your hired guns out of my way. Have them look out for any more whores trying to sneak up on me. If they'd done that yesterday, Adams would not be breathing today."

"Fine," Harden snarled as he got to his feet. "But I'm overseeing this one myself. I find my people work better when they've got someone looking over their—"

"Watch your tongue, old man," Raven interrupted. "I am not on your payroll and I do not take orders from you. It would be wise for you to remember that."

Harden nodded and then stepped around his desk. Every muscle in his body got more tense the closer he got to Raven. His teeth clenched and he quickened his pace to get around the lithe figure, but he soon realized there was no cause for alarm. Not right then, anyway.

"You do whatever you want then," Harden said. "I don't want Adams in my place of business, so I'll kick his ass out myself. Max, round up Henry and the others and be quick about it. Do you know where Abe is?"

At the merest mention of the redhead's name, Max swore he could smell the acrid scent of the opium den in his nostrils. "Yes, sir. If he's not at the jail like he's supposed to be, I have a pretty good idea of where to look."

"Then get him, too. I don't care if you have to run the whole damn way."

Max took off and bolted down the hall as though his tail had been set on fire.

Harden turned to say one last thing to Raven, but only found empty space where the other man had been standing. Quickly turning to look both ways down the hall as well as into his office, Harden was unable to find a trace of Raven, so he cursed under his breath and headed for the stairs.

From the moment he parted company with Motega, Clint put every one of his senses on the alert. The walk to the Oriental Palace seemed to take twice as long, but he studied each and every face along the way, preparing himself for anything that might be thrown at him.

Although Clint spotted a few familiar faces scowling at

him once he crossed into the Chinese district, none of those people made a move. They were undoubtedly waiting for orders, and Clint had no doubt those orders would be given very soon.

He'd spotted Max staring down at him with wide, surprised eyes from a window on the second floor just as he'd reached the Palace. Stepping through the double doors, Clint stepped so his back was against a wall and held his position right there where he could see as much as possible.

It was only a matter of seconds before a tall man with a thick mane of silvery gray hair appeared at the top of the staircase.

"Well, what have we here?" Harden said, glowering down at Clint from his perch. "The great Clint Adams comes to see me in person?"

"I tried to see you yesterday," Clint answered. "But you thought it would be better to dump me into a trap. Well, I made it out of there as you can see and I still want to talk to you."

"About that Injun? I'll pay you your money if you'd like to hand him over."

"Too late for that. I'm here for Xiang Po."

"The old man? Whatever for?"

"Because he's a human being. In case you weren't aware of it, this country has been frowning on slavery for a while now."

"That Chinaman came here using borrowed money," Harden said. "He hasn't worked it off yet. It doesn't matter how old he is, I can't have my property up and walking off when they feel like it. It's not good for my reputation."

"So that's all he is to you? Property? You really think your reputation will benefit by you tracking down some poor old man and sticking him some in some cell to rot? That doesn't do anyone a bit of good."

"Wrong. That old man belongs to me just like all these

whores belong to me. I'd track down any of these bitches if they tried to leave me, and I can't have nobody come in here to take away what's mine. Not the law and not even The Gunsmith."

"Then it looks like we've got a problem here."

Pausing for a second, Harden seemed to get distracted by something he'd only just spotted on the floor below. "No, Mr. Adams. It seems like you are the one with the problem. At least it's a problem you're already very familiar with."

Clint sensed movement to his side, but he turned just enough to look out of the corner of his eye. All of the women in the lobby of the Palace had found someplace safer to go, leaving the room all but deserted. The only movement that Clint could see was coming from the front door. He couldn't make out details, but he could see the slick, coal black hair just fine.

"Come, Mr. Adams," Raven said. "Let's be done with this."

FORTY-FOUR

Motega had spent the previous night prowling from shadow to shadow, learning every inch of Padre's Crossing while catching a few moments' sleep when he could. Therefore, he was able to get to the jail without once crossing a major street.

Along the way, he pooled up all the energies inside of him and spoke silently to the Spirit World for guidance. He didn't know if his father heard his words or not and wasn't about to wait for any kind of sign. Instead, he sped toward the jail and prepared himself for the trials ahead.

Approaching slowly, Motega was expecting many possible things. What he saw, however, managed to catch him by surprise. None of Harden's men were standing outside the jail. There wasn't even a hint of movement coming from inside the building. More than that, the door to the jail was halfway open and swinging in the breeze, idly banging against the wall.

Trying to get a better look inside, Motega kept moving forward. What struck him the most was that there didn't seem to be a single soul inside that place. He knew he'd seen Master Po taken there, and had even seen where the

guards were posted. But there were no guards in or around
that building that he could see.

Motega was crossing the street now, waiting for whoever might ambush him to make their move. So far, the
only thing moving was that door, which rocked lazily
back and forth on its hinges.

He stepped up onto the boardwalk and right up to the
door, holding a hand out to catch it as it swung toward
him. As his fingers closed around the edge, Motega saw
that the guards were indeed still inside the jail. They just
weren't quite in the same spots as when he'd seen them
last.

One of the guards was lying flat on his back on the floor.
Another was slumped against a wall close to the door and
the third was wedged half in and half out of the cell that had
previously been occupied by Master Po.

Since the jail was basically one open room, sectioned
off by bars, Motega didn't have to step in any farther to
know that his master was gone. He could see all there was
to see, and the old Chinese man was nowhere to be found.
He did see, however, that the man lying on the floor
wasn't just a guard.

That man was bigger than the rest and had a head full
of scraggly red hair.

Motega approached the large figure, staring down at
Abe's unconscious face. Stepping as though he was trying
to sneak up on a resting viper, the Indian looked for any
sign of life. He had to know if Master Po had defeated
the bigger man as well as all of these guards. If the men
were dead, then it could very well have been Raven who
set the old man free.

Then again, if it was Raven, there was no guarantee
that Master Po would be in any better condition.

Stopping so that he could look straight down at the big
man, Motega still could not tell for sure if Abe was dead
or alive. He thought for a moment that he saw Abe's chest

rise, but he couldn't be sure. He didn't take his eyes from the other man's face as he reached down to feel for any breath coming from Abe's mouth or nose.

Suddenly, Motega saw Abe move. The big man's arm snapped up and his hand reached out to clamp around Motega's wrist. Abe let out a vicious snarl as he surged into motion, but he was nowhere close to quick enough to catch Motega off-guard.

Motega pulled his arm back with lightning speed and sprung upright as Abe rolled over and lifted himself to his feet. Motega could hardly believe that the redhead was moving at all. Abe's jaw was swollen to twice its normal size and both his eyes were blackened. The knife wound on his side was dark with crusted blood and sticking to his skin.

"Virst I'm gonna kill you," Abe snarled through his mutilated jaw. "Then I'm gonna kill that vucking god-damn old jinaman vriend of yours."

Abe swung wildly with one fist while reaching for the gun at his side with the other. The first punch fell short as Motega ducked back and out of the way; it swung past the Indian like a log at the end of a rope.

Every one of Motega's instincts said to stay and fight, just as his father would have done. But Motega thought back to his other father and what the old Chinese man would have recommended. Master Po would have opted for a wiser path, which was what Motega and Clint had already worked out.

Filled with the rage of a beast, Abe lashed out again, with a swing so powerful it might have lopped Motega's head from his shoulders. That one didn't connect either, which didn't concern Abe too much since his gun was now in hand.

Motega swallowed his pride, thought back to what he and Clint had discussed, and ran.

Letting out a feral howl, Abe took off after him.

FORTY-FIVE

Clint stepped through the door of the Oriental Palace. His eyes were focused on Raven, but he paid close attention to his peripheral vision as well. Whenever he saw another one of Harden's men trying to get closer, all Clint had to do was throw a quick glare in the man's direction to back him off.

Raven hopped down from the boardwalk and stood in the middle of the street. Turning around to face Clint, he said, "Isn't this where you prefer to do your killing? In the middle of the street like all the other gunfighters?"

"I don't know. Perhaps we could go into a back room where you'd feel more comfortable."

"It doesn't matter how you die," Raven said. "You are not why I am here."

"That's right. You prefer to kill elderly men who used to treat you like their blood kin. That's why you're here, right?"

Raven stared at Clint for a moment before his lips curled into a smile. "Master Po? He is part of my reason for being here, but no bigger part than that loudmouthed fool who struts around inside that whorehouse. Harden

179

and Po have served their purpose, but now you stand in between me and the ultimate goal."

"You're after Motega?"

For a moment, it seemed as though Raven's eyes had ignited into small pyres. But they died down quickly and he regained his composure. "Harden wanted to show he could reclaim his slave, so I helped him because I knew that would bring Motega here to me. That redskin took the spot that should have been mine. Master Po's teachings could have elevated me to become a master myself. Instead, he decided to spend his remaining years with that Indian.

"When I tried to be the good son and regain my spirit father's favor, I was spurned. I saved their lives, Mr. Adams. More times than they know, I saved them both from men that were after their skins. And instead of thanks, I get asked to never show my face around them again.

"I cannot bring myself to kill Master Po. His years and mind are waning anyway. But it is Motega who deserves death even more. He dares to turn my master away from me, even after I killed to save them both. For that, he will die and Master Po will have to walk alone for what little time he has left."

Clint moved as Raven moved; the two of them walking in a circle so they always remained the same distance apart. Every so often, Raven would snap his head forward, taunting Clint and smiling when he saw the other man twitch.

"I'll beat you again," Raven said. "Just as I did before. The way of the Empty Hand is far more deadly than any machine, no matter how fast you can use that device."

At that moment, both men saw a figure bolting from a nearby alley. It was Motega and he was running as swiftly as an elk. Immediately, the Indian changed his course so that he was running straight toward Raven.

Raven planted his feet and held his hands open and low

at his sides. "Take your swing, little spirit brother," Raven taunted. "Because it appears as though you will soon have your hands full."

Sure enough, Abe was just then charging out of the same alley. He thundered over the cold dirt like a bull, his head held low and his fist wrapped around his .44. The redhead pumped his legs beneath him, the smell of his prey fresh in his nose.

A shot cracked through the air, kicking up a mound of dirt at Abe's feet, which stopped the big man cold.

"If it's all the same to you," Clint said, "I think we'll switch up. You two can settle things your own way and I'll take care of the big fella here. I think my crude device will handle him just fine."

Abe's nostrils flared and his eyes became wide and crazed. He shifted to look at Clint and took a couple steps forward. "Vuck you, too, Adams. You're nothin' to me."

Clint didn't say a word. He could tell by looking at him that Abe was not a man to be reasoned with. He would either back down or come ahead no matter what Clint said to him. So Clint stood his ground, dropped the Colt back into its holster and waited.

The instant Motega saw that Abe was no longer after him, he set his sights on Raven. The men approached each other slowly, bowed, and then threw themselves at each other with a flurry of fists and feet. They moved so fast and connected so many times that Clint couldn't keep track of who was doing damage and who was blocking.

Trusting Motega to handle the situation, Clint focused all his attention on Abe.

As the redhead got closer, Clint could see the clouded haze in his eyes. Abe was obviously either drunk or under some other influence to continue functioning with so much damage done to his body. It was no wonder Motega hadn't been able to drop him. It would be a long time before the bigger man felt any pain at all.

"Virst I'll kill you," Abe sneered. "Then I'll kill them jinamen you like so much."

At that moment, Clint heard something that drew his attention away from Abe. It was the metallic click of a pistol's hammer being drawn back and it was coming from the building behind him. Waiting until the last moment, Clint twisted around on the balls of his feet as his hand plucked the Colt from his side.

When he'd completed his turn, Clint took a fraction of a second to look at what was behind him. He saw Harden standing in the double doors to the Oriental Palace, aiming a pistol at Clint's chest.

In the next fraction of a second, Clint had pulled his trigger and was already turning back around as the bullet punched a hole through Harden's skull. He could hear Harden dropping onto the floor as he put Abe back into his field of vision.

The redhead was fast for such a big man. He had already lifted his gun and was taking aim by the time Clint was facing him. Not wasting another moment, Clint squeezed off a round that grazed Abe's wrist and bounced off his gun hand enough to push Abe's pistol down and to one side as the big man pulled his trigger.

Clint could hear Abe's round hissing within inches of his head as he took aim and put a bullet of his own into Abe's chest.

The lead punched through Abe's ribs, sending a spout of blood into the air. But the big man refused to drop and was even lifting his hand to take another shot at Clint.

Not quite believing what he was seeing, Clint put another bullet straight through Abe's heart, one through his left eye and his last round through his forehead.

A crimson mist of blood and brain matter hung around Abe's head as his eyes wavered and glazed over. For a moment, Clint thought the other man was still going to stay upright, and he quickly emptied the Colt's cylinder so he could reload. Before he got the first fresh round in its place, however, Clint watched Abe's eyes roll up into his head and his body drop lifelessly to the ground.

He then turned his attention toward Motega and Raven. Their hands were flying at each other with lightning speed, striking and blocking and then counterstriking in a never-ending flow of motion. Finally, Motega twisted away, reached behind him and removed the arrow that was sheathed on his back.

The arrow flashed through the air, following up on a punch he'd thrown with his other hand. When he snapped the arrow forward, the flow of motion stopped.

Raven's upper body drooped and his arms swung limply from his shoulders. Gazing down at the arrow that was in his chest, he hacked up a bloody cough. He then looked up to Motega and said, "That is not the path . . . of the . . . Empty Hand."

Motega kept his eyes focused on Raven's, as though he could stare all the way into the other man's soul. "Master Po taught us to know one's enemy and adapt rather than be overcome," the Indian said. "If you'd have listened to his wisdom, you would have known that, too."

With that, Motega pushed the arrowhead in farther, twisted it and then pulled it out in one powerful wrenching motion. The arrow came free amid a spray of blood, opening Raven's chest and spilling his life into the dirt.

"Let's get to your teacher before the rest of Harden's men do," Clint said after reloading and snapping the Colt shut with a flick of his wrist.

Motega looked up and shook his head. "Do not concern yourself, friend. Master Po has escaped on his own, and I doubt the body of this little group will continue fighting now that its head has been severed."

Clint looked around and saw that Harden's gunmen were making themselves scarce and tossing their weapons down behind them. "Yeah. You may be right about that.

Mopping them up is the sheriff's job anyway." When Clint looked back to Motega, he saw that the Indian was walking away as well.

"Hey," Clint said. "Where are you going?"

The Indian stopped and looked over his shoulder. "To find my master. He will need my help now that he is once again on his own. He is also my family. A man should not stray too far from his family."

"Good luck, Motega," Clint said. "When you find him, give Master Po my regards. He sounds like my kind of guy."

"Hey, what the hell—" a man's voice called.

Clint turned and saw a man with a badge walking toward him. He didn't know where the sheriff had been all this time, but he knew he was going to have to explain some things to him.

He turned to wave one more time to Motega, but the Indian was gone.

Watch for

THE LOVE OF MONEY

264th novel in the exciting GUNSMITH series
from Jove

Coming in December!

Explore the exciting Old West with one of the men who made it wild!

**AVAILABLE WHEREVER BOOKS ARE SOLD OR
TO ORDER CALL:
1-800-788-6262**

(Ad # B112)

WILDGUN

THE HARD-DRIVING WESTERN SERIES
FROM THE CREATORS OF *LONGARM*

Jack Hanson

Round 'em all up!

Available wherever books are sold or
to order call 1-800-788-6262

B061